W9-BNK-394

FIGHTING

EL FUEGO

BY

PETE BIRLE

el fuego is Spanish for "the fire."

Fighting El Fuego. COPYRIGHT 2005
by Pete Birle
All rights reserved. Printed in China.
No part of this book may be used or
reproduced in any manner whatsoever without
written permission, except in the case of brief
quotations embodied in critical articles and reviews.
For information about Scobre...

Scobre Press Corporation
2255 Calle Clara
La Jolla, CA 92037

Scobre Press books may be purchased for
educational, business or sales promotional use.

Edited by Helen Glenn Court
Illustrated by Gail Piazza
Cover Design by Michael Lynch

ISBN 1-933423-29-3

TOUCHDOWN EDITION

www.scobre.com

CHAPTER ONE

EL FUEGO

"How's that feel?" A lean black man in his late sixties wraps another layer of tape tight around my right hand. I make a fist and slam it into the open palm of my left. The thwack it makes lets me know that the taping job is first-rate.

"Feels good," I answer, sliding off the training table and standing upright. I begin throwing quick punches at an imaginary opponent. Shadowboxing, as it's called, is the best way to warm up before a fight. I throw several hard jabs into the air, calming my nerves a bit every time my arm extends.

"Stand still," the man says firmly. I stop in my tracks as he begins to apply a thin coat of Vaseline to my face. I hate the slippery feel of the Vaseline. Still, I know how important it is, so I try not to move while he rubs it in. In a few minutes, I'll be glad it's there. When my opponent hits my face, his glove will slide on the Vaseline rather than connect solidly with my head. "This goo is gonna help you from ending up with a face

like mine," the old man laughs, revealing a crooked smile with several missing teeth. I glance past his mouth and up at his twisted nose, which looks to have been broken a few times.

I force a smile, wondering if my face will ever get worn down the way his has over the years. "Thanks," I say softly.

He nods his head in a knowing way and then winks at me before saying, "Don't worry, kid, you ain't gonna end up as ugly as me." The calm look on his face in the middle of these tense moments reflects a serenity that can only come from a lifetime in the ring. I smile again, for real this time.

Throughout this process, a serious-faced official watches over us, making sure that all my preparations are legal. As I throw a few more jabs into the air, and finish off a combination with a hard uppercut, I think about my parents and my coach and my brother. Suddenly my heart is racing. I realize in this moment how desperately I want to win this one. Not just for me, but for all of them.

Once finished with the pre-fight preparations, the old man puts down his roll of tape and jar of grease. He picks up a pair of gloves, which he proceeds to shove onto my hands. He laces them up, tight, and slaps them hard with his hands when he is finished. The room is now eerily quiet. I begin hopping around again, throwing more punches into the air. My hands are adjusting to the feeling of the gloves more and more with every moment. After a few minutes, I can't even feel the gloves—they have become extensions of my hands. I am now completely focused, ready to fight.

"Stay still," the old man repeats to me. "We're not finished." I stop moving again as he helps me into my headgear.

The padded helmet that amateur boxers wear for protection fits snugly on my head. After strapping it on, he steps out of the way so that the official can approve his handiwork. As he turns to leave, he shouts powerfully over his shoulder in Spanish, "Buena suerte." Good luck to you. I nod my head.

I watch as the former boxer-turned-trainer makes his way toward the exit. The room is once again completely quiet—exactly the way I like it before a bout. But, unfortunately, the old man has to open the door to get out. When he does, all the noise from the crowded arena pours in on me. It's loud out there, and though the cheering gets my adrenaline pumping, I look forward to the door closing and the silence returning.

The door clicks closed and I am alone with the official. He opens up a folding chair and takes a seat in the far corner of the locker room. I start to throw a few more punches into the air, practicing a powerful combination. I know that this fight will take all of my strength, and with it every ounce of control that I can muster. For a boxer to be successful in the ring, he needs to control his emotions and stick to his game plan. Fighting on adrenaline does not work in the ring. I learned this lesson as a kid, and I learned it the hard way.

My breathing is a little heavier now and I know that I have done a decent job warming up. I can hear my heart beating and nothing else. I'm eighteen years old and getting ready to fight in the Box-offs here at the Olympic Training Center in Colorado Springs. This building is the home of the U.S. Olympic team. Just being here is a dream come true. But I'm nowhere near content stopping now. I want to make the team, represent my country, and bring home a gold medal. In just five minutes I am going to be fighting the most important fight of my life. It will determine my fate as an Olympic boxer. If I win, I go to the Summer Games in San Jose, Costa Rica. If I lose, I go home.

I've already won at the U.S. Championships, the Eastern Trials, and the Olympic Team Trials. Still, to make the U.S. Olympic boxing team and compete for a medal, I've got to win one more.

There's no denying that I'm in the best shape of my life. At five feet, seven inches tall and a solid 140 pounds, I'm vying to become the U.S. representative in the light welterweight division.

My opponent is the nephew of a former world champion, who held the professional junior middleweight title for several years. Most of the reporters and newspapers are predicting his victory over me. This doesn't faze me. I know exactly what I have to do to win, and I plan on doing it.

A long mirror hangs crookedly on the back wall of the tiny room I'm waiting in. I walk past the silent official and over to the mirror. When I get about a foot away from it, I take a good long look at myself. First, I glance down at my white shorts with the blue striped beltline. Then I stare at my white tank top and down at my red sneakers. Although I proudly wear the colors of the American flag, I know the same colors also represent Puerto Rico—the country where my parents were born and the place most of my relatives still call home. These colors constantly remind me of my responsibility to my family and the two countries I love.

For me, life wasn't always as exciting as it is tonight. I hadn't always felt a love of country, or even a love of myself. There was a time when I could never have imagined representing anything or pursuing any kind of goal, especially such a lofty one as becoming an Olympic athlete. Back in the day, I didn't have any dreams. I didn't even know who I was. I was lost. If you knew me when I was a kid, you would never have believed that I could have made it this far.

Standing a few feet from the mirror, I stare into my dark brown eyes. I look past the pupils, deep into my heart. "There you are," I whisper. "El Fuego." I can still see it in my eyes— the white hot fire, the beast. Although I've learned to control it over the years, by long ago burying it somewhere deep inside of myself, I know that fire is still dangerous. And I know that I will always have to keep an eye on it. Because once ignited, el fuego will burn out of control, and take me down with it.

When I was a kid, anger ran my life. I never knew when an explosion was coming. Once it started—once el fuego took hold—I couldn't do anything to stop it. It was a living thing. It breathed. It ate. It hated. And it nearly ruined my life. It was a long time before I realized that I couldn't kill this fire raging inside me. It was part of me. I had to live with it. I had to learn to tame it.

In the middle of this thought, the locker room door opens again. I turn away from the mirror as the noise from the crowd takes over the tiny room. This time the door stays opened wide. I put my robe on and throw a few jabs into the air. I stare out toward the lights of the arena. Now my heart is really racing. Smack! I hit my gloves together and turn toward the doorway.

The old man speaks to me. "Let's go, kid, fight night."

CHAPTER TWO

RECESS

My name is Francisco Diaz. Only I didn't like being called Francisco when I was twelve. I didn't like being called Francis, Frankie, or Frank, either. I went by my nickname, Paco. And when I told someone to call me Paco, I meant it.

Although I was born in the United States—in Philadelphia— my folks were both from the island of Puerto Rico. They moved to Philly right after they got married. A few years later, when they decided to start a family, they moved down to Rock River, which is across the Delaware River from New Jersey. We've been here ever since.

Like many American-born Hispanics, I'm bilingual. I'm not saying that this makes me a genius, it just is what it is. When I was little, my parents were always speaking Spanish around the house. Even though we lived in Pennsylvania, Spanish was the first language I spoke. By the time I got to kindergarten, though, I was speaking perfect English, too. Dad said I learned my English from watching a lot of television, but I can remember hundreds of conversations with my older brother that helped me along as well. It was just like Dad to forget details that involved my brother.

I looked like your average Rock River sixth-grader: black hair, skinny, and short with strong Latin features. I may have looked a lot like the other kids at St. Joe's Elementary School—the private school I had been attending for two months after being expelled from my last school—but I sure didn't act like them. I can still remember one incident on the playground that really singled me out as a problem child. It also ended up changing my life.

His name was Butchie LaManna and he thought he was hot stuff. He was two grades ahead of me. Butchie was the typical eighth-grade bully, preying on anyone smaller and weaker. He'd approach the younger kids on the playground and scare them into giving up their basketball or handing over their baseball cards. He did that kind of thing pretty much every day.

Of course, Butchie always had two of his buddies with him. Like every other bully I knew, he needed the muscle behind him. My guess was that he couldn't provide it himself. I'd never gotten involved with those three, because they never really bothered me. I looked at Butchie and his crew as a minor annoyance, something I could avoid pretty easily. After all, I had no friends and kept pretty much to myself back then.

One afternoon in early October, Butchie made a huge mistake. He also made my plan of ignoring him fall to pieces. He had obviously heard about my reputation as a troublemaker, as a kid you didn't want to mess with. This reputation had followed me to St. Joe's. This reputation also made me a target for Butchie. In his mind, taking me down would raise his stature among the other students—fortifying his position as the toughest kid in school.

During my first month or so at St. Joe's, I felt Butchie staring at me constantly. I did my best not to make eye contact with him, though I could tell he was sizing me up. I think we both knew that eventually we were going to bump into one another.

I was minding my own business that day, leaning against the fence in the corner of the playground. Standing alone at recess was not uncommon for me. I would regularly look at a comic book and watch the rest of the kids talking and playing ball. I never joined them. One, I was never asked. Two, I wouldn't have said yes even if I had been. I was a loner, not necessarily because I wanted to be one, but because I just was. I'm not really sure why. I do know that if someone tried to get close to me, it usually didn't take long for them to say something that would set me off. Then I'd push them away—literally. I saw my fair share of the principal's office because I was constantly getting into fights. In short, I was a mixed up, high-strung, angry kid, and everyone with an opinion told me so. So I just went with it.

I really didn't know how messed up I was until Butchie approached me that day.

"Hey, Diaz!" Butchie called out, walking toward me with his two stooges, Tommy and Ray Ray, following close behind.

I tried to ignore him but he wouldn't quit. "I'm talking to you, Pah-coh!" he said, louder this time, clearly trying to mimic a stereotypical Hispanic accent.

Just about everyone on the playground heard him—and almost all of them stopped what they were doing to watch. Even the girls who were practicing their double-dutch jump-roping stopped—and those girls never stopped.

Butchie had addressed me by my last name and then again by my nickname. It would have been rude not to respond. As if I cared. I had already made a career—and not just in school—of being rude. I said nothing. I wasn't interested in a conversation. I didn't care what the consequences of ignoring him were.

"Are you deaf or something?" asked Butchie. "Or are you just really stupid?" This comment caused his pair of goons to break into laughter.

I remember looking up at him blankly. I stood staring into his eyes, the anger building up inside me. At that point, I couldn't think about anything besides slamming my fist into Butchie's face. My right hand started to curl into a tight ball. My left hand followed a moment later. If he could have read my mind, he would have stopped messing with me. If he could have seen what I was seeing in my head, he would have turned around and bothered someone else. But he didn't.

The funny thing was that I wasn't a big kid. I was actually kind of scrawny back then. My small frame and unkempt black hair made me look like a geek, too, or at least a pushover. Yet, even at twelve years old, I was strong. I was like a compact volcano of energy. When I was mad, I mean really mad, I would erupt. As Butchie continued moving closer to me, things were really starting to rumble inside of me.

"I'm talking to you, Diaz," he continued. The bully was now inches away from me. He and his friends were determined to see this thing through. "You have something I want."

I knew he expected me to ask, "What?" so that he could respond with some clever remark, which in the end wouldn't be that clever. Even though I knew he was talking about the comic book I was holding, I wasn't going to say anything. It helped that I was so blinded by rage at this point that I couldn't speak even if I had wanted to. All I could do was glare at Butchie. I could feel my heart rate quicken. The rumble inside of me was getting louder and louder. The sound was like an approaching train—and Butchie was standing on the tracks. To be honest, it was getting harder and harder to ignore.

"Everybody's right, you are a wacko." Butchie shook his head from side to side as he spoke, occasionally glancing at Tommy and Ray Ray. He smiled from ear to ear when he said, "I just wanted to see your comic book for a minute, Diaz. Now it looks like I'm going to have to take it from you and keep it for myself." He looked back over at Tommy and Ray Ray. "Don't worry. He's not so tough. Are you Pah-coh?" As he spoke these words he reached out to grab the comic book from my hand.

In the instant it took Butchie to reach toward me I decided to respond—but not verbally. The rumble inside of me exploded— the train had arrived. And now that the fire was lit, there was nothing I could do to put it out.

I remember the first punch that I hit Butchie with. It was a hard right hand to his cheek. Just as I followed through, I turned toward Tommy and Ray Ray, who had already run across the playground. I wanted to give them a dose of the same medicine I was about to give Butchie, but they wouldn't have any of it. After my punch connected, I decided it was time to say something. "Looks like you're on your own, Butchie."

Raising his hands and then making two fists, he started to circle around me. This was a clear indication that he wasn't afraid to fight. "You should have just given up your comic book, Diaz,"

Butchie continued, "because now you're in big trouble."

Teachers and principals had been giving my parents the same report on me for a few years now: I lashed out and attacked others who had no real interest in fighting back. I fought dirty. I punched first. I never apologized. I was pretty much a monster.

In this case, though, my foe was willing to fight back. Unfortunately, that only fueled my fire. I was already a servant to my master—el fuego. I had neither the desire nor the ability to change my plans. I was caught in el fuego's clutches, and my destiny was predetermined. I would fight.

I recall the two of us pummeling each other—Butchie hitting me with his fists, me hitting him with my hands, my elbows, my forehead, my knees, and my feet. Every time Butchie would get in a well-timed punch that caught me off-guard, I would retaliate like a madman. Although he was much bigger than me, I was landing the majority of the punches. I can't remember the specifics, because things would get fuzzy for me when I was in the middle of a fight. The rage and the fury, which my mom said was the expression of my frustration, took over, and I would operate on impulse. On blind instinct. Like a cornered animal. It was scary.

The truth was that I had no control over myself. And during this dark time in my life, I really hated myself. I think deep down, I wanted to get better. I just didn't know how.

As the fight unfolded, many of the kids on the playground looked scared or upset. Some turned their heads. Even the more curious, who were brave enough to inch closer, had strange expressions on their faces. They looked disturbed by what they were witnessing. It was the playground version of a carnival, and I was the freak that attracted all the pointing and staring.

And yet, despite my fury, Butchie was no pushover. He may very well have been scared, but he didn't show it. We had started to fight next to the fence. Just a few seconds later, we'd moved over to the swing set. I recall Butchie popping me in the face with his left. After that, I tried to grab him, in the hope of wrestling him to the ground. But I couldn't force his big body onto the pavement. Every time I got a hold of his shirt or his pants, he would step back and hit me in the chest.

I remember feeling that pain, around my eye from his left hook and along my chest from his many punches. Instead of respecting the source of that pain, I disregarded it, letting el fuego overrule logic. It was my rage that enabled me to finally knock Butchie down, albeit with a swift and sneaky kick to the groin. Once he was doubled over on the blacktop, I didn't back off. Although part of me knew I shouldn't, the rest of me couldn't stop. After kicking him a few times while he lay on the asphalt, I got ready to stomp.

Mr. Bermudez, the fifth-grade teacher on duty at recess that day, finally made it over to stop the fight. He was sixty-one years old and dressed in a brown suit and tie. He had to run all the way across the playground to reach us.

Now, this next part I don't remember. I was told about it later, when Principal Grace asked me to sit in on a meeting with her and my parents. When Mr. Bermudez arrived, I was apparently standing over Butchie, and I was just about to jump on his head. El fuego was burning, and I was obviously still crazed. Which is why, when Mr. Bermudez reached out to pull me away from Butchie, I latched on to St. Joe's oldest and most respected teacher like a pit bull—and bit him on the arm.

CHAPTER THREE

A BAD SEED

As principal of St. Joe's Elementary, Mrs. Grace had a file on every student. It didn't take her long to find mine. It did take her a while to pull it out of her desk, though, because it was pretty thick. St. Joe's was my third school in three years. My parents had hoped that the discipline and special attention it provided would address the problems I had at the last two public schools I attended.

Sitting and poking my newly acquired black eye with my finger, I looked at Mrs. Grace. Then, I looked at my folks. I guessed that St. Joe's wasn't the answer.

"Francisco," she began.

I immediately interrupted her. "My name is Paco," I said. My mother sighed. My father shot me a look of disapproval.

Mrs. Grace seemed to ignore my comment. I looked across the desk at the old lady, dressed in a black and white suit. I know I should have respected her position as principal of the school, but I couldn't. She looked up at me, her eyes devoid of the warmth they usually conveyed. "This is the final straw, Francisco," she said, her voice ringing with a pitch that was entirely out of her usual character. "The way you acted today was simply disgraceful." For the first time since I met her, Mrs. Grace sounded mean.

I looked down at my shoes, which still had some of Butchie's blood on them.

She continued talking. "Not only was this the fourth fight you've been in since joining us six weeks ago, but this is also the second teacher you've assaulted. I'm not even going to discuss the disrespect you've displayed in the classroom and the foul behavior you exhibit when angry. You have all the makings of a bad seed, young man," she added, her voice taking on an even sharper tone. "You need the proper nourishment to grow, and that must happen now, before it's too late and you do real harm—to yourself or others."

I knew what was coming. My dad had said it when he and Mom enrolled me at St. Joe's. One more invitation for them to come in and see the principal and my next stop would be a twelve-month tour of duty at a military school in Ohio.

"Your father has mentioned a military school to me, and under the circumstances, I don't think it's a bad idea." Mrs. Grace leaned forward. "However, you might end up getting kicked out of there as well, and then where would we turn?" She sighed deeply. "So until we can find out what is making you behave this way, we'll keep you here," she said, "even if it means under lock and key."

Turning to my parents, she concluded, "I think we should at least see what we're dealing with here before anyone moves ahead and does something drastic. That's why," she turned back to me, "I'm recommending you see a psychologist. We need to figure out why you're acting this way."

My older brother JoJo and I were inseparable. We did everything together. We walked to school together. We rode bikes together. We went to the movies together. We shared the same room—our toys and clothes—our fears and dreams. We were best friends.

José Diaz, which is my brother's real name, was my hero. To me, JoJo was the greatest guy in the world. He found time to hang out with me, teach me things, and tell me jokes. I always wanted to be around him, and he didn't mind me tagging along most of the time. I think he even enjoyed it.

I knew that I wanted to grow up to be just like him. And then, one day, he was gone. Out of my life forever. Just like that. Two policemen knocked on the door to our apartment one night during dinner, grabbed my brother, shoved him down the staircase, and sat him in the back seat of their car. I stood there crying as they drove away with him. I never saw him again. He was fifteen. I was eight.

It turns out that JoJo had joined a local gang. To become a member, he had committed a crime—a serious crime, a violent crime. Because of that he was sent away to prison for a long time.

My parents disowned him. At my father's command, his name was never to be spoken in our apartment again. Whatever pictures there were of JoJo were taken down, boxed up, and either thrown away or put in the closet. My baby sister Marisol was only three when JoJo left. By the time she turned five, she hardly remembered him.

But I did. I remembered him. I thought about him every day—from the night he was taken away, to the day he was tried, to the afternoon he was sentenced, to the morning he went off to prison. And every day since.

Before JoJo was locked up, I was a pretty normal kid. Sure, I could be excitable at times, but I was no trouble. I was your typical second-grader. Even when all of this trouble unfolded with my brother, I didn't freak out—not right away at least. Except for becoming quieter and more reserved, I was dealing fairly well with the shame of my brother being a criminal. I was doing the best I could under the circumstances: my best friend up and leaving me, and my parents pretending he never existed. I was okay. For a while, that is.

A year later, by the time I was nine, things were changing. I started to feel really angry about what happened to JoJo. I was angry at the police for taking him away. I was angry at the gang for recruiting him. I was angry at him for leaving me. I was angry at my parents for disowning him. I felt like nothing really mattered—that my life was insignificant, forgotten, forsaken, like a piece of garbage in a landfill. So I stopped caring about doing the right thing. I stopped being polite. I stopped smiling all the time and laughing at funny jokes. I stopped trying to make friends, hugging my mother, respecting my father, doing well in school, or calling my grandmother on her birthday. None of that mattered to me.

I was on my own, and the best way to protect myself from getting hurt again was to stop caring about anything or anyone—including myself.

CHAPTER FOUR

KILLER INSTINCT

So this was it, I remember thinking, as I exited my parents' car. My next stop wasn't going to be the Army. It was here, at a shrink's office.

Dr. Adriana Colón was a former St. Joe's student who went on to complete high school in three years, then college, then medical school. She had always been a favorite of Mrs. Grace, especially since she came back to Rock River to practice child psychology in her old neighborhood. Smart and attractive, with long black hair and stylish glasses, Dr. Colón was the pride of Rock River's Puerto Rican community. At the moment, I seemed to be the curse.

She was waiting for us at the top of a spiraling staircase when we arrived. As I approached the front door to her office, I was still thinking about what my dad had said moments earlier, as we made our way toward the two-story building: "If this doesn't work, you will be in a Hill Valley Military School uniform by next semester." I had to admit that the thought of attending military school

17

scared me.

Like I said, I think that deep down, I wanted to change. Not just because I was scared of being sent away, but because being out of control was a scary thing in itself. Life was no fun for me. I had nobody and nothing. Still, as far as I was concerned, there wasn't anything I could do to tame el fuego.

My parents and I walked into a small waiting room which led to an office. "Good afternoon," Dr. Colòn said, extending her hand for me to shake. "You must be Paco." I was surprised and somewhat satisfied that the doctor chose to call me by the name I preferred. Nevertheless, I avoided eye contact when I shook her hand.

"Señor y señora Diaz, gracias. Mucho gusto," she said to my folks in Spanish, shaking each of their hands as well. "You two can wait here while Paco and I talk in my office."

All of a sudden, I didn't feel too well. Regardless of her attempt to get on my good side, just being in a psychologist's office was making me sick. I knew right away that this lady was probably going to ask me a lot of questions about my feelings. I really hated talking about my feelings.

As I followed Dr. Colòn into the warmly decorated room, with soft couches, fresh flowers, and bright wallpaper, I glanced back at my folks. The pained expression on my face caused my mom to respond with a look of reassurance. My dad just glared at me. I'm not sure if his stare meant, "Now, don't mess this up," or if it was an indication of how disappointed he was in me. Either way, when my eyes met his, I immediately looked to the floor with shame.

I knew he was disappointed in me—really disappointed. My dad, a roofer and part-time builder, was a man's man. He was wiry with long arms, but his body was hardened, just like his will. And he was as strong as an ox. I once saw him lift our refrigerator straight up in the air, when Mom lost her wedding ring underneath it. He never let his emotions get the best of him. He thought that a person's ability to refrain from blowing their cool was their greatest strength. He also thought that people who acted out physically when pushed were weak. This was why he reacted so harshly to JoJo's arrest, and this is why the thought of me having to see a therapist was beyond his comprehension. To him, my brother and I both possessed something that he didn't—some weakness, some defect, that led us to act out. I was really starting to think that my father resented me. Like everything else in my life, this made me angry.

He, much more than my mom, was at his wits' end. I heard him tell my mother that exact thing two nights earlier. At this time in my life, my father and I had a pretty bad relationship. I often wondered if he even wanted me to get better. I believe now, that in addition to not wanting to go against Mrs. Grace's professional opinion, he did want to see my life improve. He desperately wanted to fix in me what he couldn't fix in JoJo. I know now that Dad loved me, though he certainly didn't know how to show it back then.

Of course, my mother was my on my side—she always had been. She didn't agree with the philosophy my father believed in—contempt and frequent punishment. She continued to encourage me no matter how badly I behaved. I didn't find out until later, but she never wanted to take down the pictures of JoJo. Secretly, she wrote him letters she mailed without my father's knowledge. Thinking about it now, I realize that my brother and I really crushed our mother's spirit with our poor behavior and bad choices. She was sad all the time. Her two sons had been the light of her life just a few years earlier. Now, with JoJo gone and me acting out, all she knew was grief and despair.

In my heart, I realized how badly Mom wanted her smiling, happy son back. Every time I looked at her I felt guilty. But still, showing her any love was impossible for me. I had convinced myself that the loving boy she was looking for was gone.

My parents had a lot of arguments about me, stemming largely from their different approaches to my so-called issues. More and more, I was the topic of conversation at the dinner table. I was the subject of the shouting I heard coming from their bedroom both early in the morning and late at night. I can't even begin to estimate how many times I heard my father say to my mother, "You don't want him to turn out like the other one, do you?" They had been in enough principals' offices, too, and were getting tired of making visits to my schools. They were hoping that this psychologist could make some sense out of me.

"So, Paco," Dr. Colòn asked, sitting down across from me in a big armchair. "How are you today?"

I had sat down on the couch opposite her. The office reminded me of a living room, not a doctor's office, but I still didn't feel at home. I fidgeted in my seat, first bringing my knee to my chest, then placing both feet on the ground and leaning forward. I was very uncomfortable, and I'm sure that it showed. "Good," I answered, diverting my eyes. I looked out the window over Dr. Colòn's shoulder. I'd have given anything to be outside in the crisp fall air—away from this office and all my problems. I unbuttoned the top button of my shirt, as it started to get really warm in there.

"I'm glad to hear that," she said. Her voice was soothing but it didn't put me at ease—not yet. I could feel my heart starting to beat a bit faster and my armpits dampen with perspiration.

"Well," she said, grabbing a folder and a notebook from off the coffee table in front of her. She then pulled a pen from the inside pocket of her blazer. "We've got a lot to talk about, so why don't we get started?"

I started moving around in my seat again. I hated this situation. I hated being in this warm room, talking to this stranger. "Okay," I said with some uncertainty and a hint of anger in my voice. "So, what am I supposed to say? You're the doctor, right? Shouldn't you say something first?"

She smiled. "I'm much more interested in hearing from you. First of all, relax, Paco. This is not a test," Dr. Colòn said. "I just want to get to know you better. Why don't you start by telling me what you like to do?"

I didn't know what to say at first, so I just mentioned the first thing that popped into my head. "Um, I like watching baseball sometimes."

"Me too," she responded. "I'm a big Phillies fan. I hope this is the year we can finally beat out the Braves. What else do you like?"

Honestly, I wasn't a big baseball fan at all, but I had to say something. Still, hearing Dr. Colòn talk about the Phillies made me a bit more comfortable. If nothing else, it took my mind off of the fact that I was sitting in a psychologist's office. So I started talking to her more. I mentioned my comic books, a few television shows I liked, and some video games I played at home. For the next twenty minutes, I talked a lot. Dr. Colòn learned that I liked superheroes, movies about cowboys and Indians, and arroz con pollo.

In the middle of talking about this stuff, I figured something out: Dr. Colòn was buttering me up—setting me up. So, in the middle of our chat, I stopped talking as suddenly as I had started. I then looked at her with a sly smile, as if to say, "Come on, what do you really want to talk about?" That's when I started to lose control a little. It wasn't that I was surprised by what Dr. Colòn was trying to do. In fact, I knew what was happening from the start. Comic books and video games weren't the things Principal Grace sent me here to talk about. My breathing started to get heavier and I leaned up in my seat. "I'm done talking for now."

Dr. Colòn could feel my change. "Tell me what you're feeling right now, Paco. Tell me what you feel when you are about to lose control?" She asked this question matter-of-factly.

Just then, I felt a spasm in my neck as the blood rushed to my head. I had actually been stupid enough to trust this lady, but she was just like the rest of them! I was starting to get really angry. The uneasiness I had been feeling began to fuel my fire. I could feel el fuego coming. Yet, at that moment, I really didn't want to explode. Not here. That would just prove everyone right. I actually thought about that, too, which was strange for me. I took a deep breath and blurted out, "I don't know how I feel." I was trying to give an honest answer while doing my best to suppress my emotions. "I know that when I'm mad sometimes, I think about my brother. Then I kind of lose it."

"Okay," she said, reassuringly. "Let's explore that. You love your brother, huh?" To this question, I had no response. I simply stared at the wall. Dr. Colòn kept talking. "Paco, I can only help you if you talk to me. Tell me about him. Tell me why you're so angry."

This question did not make me want to storm out the door, attack Dr. Colòn, or punch a hole in the wall.

Instead, it made me think. Why *was* I so angry? I slumped down into the couch and began telling her everything—things I didn't even know about myself came out. I have to admit, it felt pretty good. After an hour of talking, mostly about JoJo and the night he was taken away in handcuffs, things seemed okay. El fuego had disappeared and I was no longer warm and uncomfortable.

When we emerged from the office, I was exhausted. My mom noticed it immediately and came over to put her arms around me. My dad wasn't so observant, but he did muster a sympathetic smile. "Well," he said, glancing at Dr. Colòn. "What do you think?"

"Why don't you all join me back in my office," Dr. Colòn said.

Once inside, I sat back on the couch, nearly falling asleep. My parents sat one on each side of me. Dr. Colòn returned to her chair. She removed her glasses and leaned forward. "We've only had one session," she said, "so I can't tell you exactly why Paco lashes out the way he does. I do think it may have a lot to do with the absence of his brother." The moment she mentioned this, my father looked toward the window, away from her. She continued, "He's a very angry young man. This anger takes hold of him sometimes, and he feels that there is nothing he can do to stop it. I believe that Paco has what's called a killer instinct."

My mother gasped. My father took a deep breath. I cringed.

"What exactly is that?" my dad asked.

"It's a condition that causes Paco to react with a burst of

fury and energy when he is angered—a burst that demands to be released," the doctor said. "I've done some studying in this area, and I can say, with some degree of confidence, that he's got it. When he gets angry, he boils over very easily. And once he starts, he can't stop himself." She smiled over at me. "Not yet, at least."

After it had sunk in, being diagnosed with such a sinister label, my mother spoke up. "So what do we do about it?"

"Well, Paco comes in to see me twice every week, and together we'll begin to tackle this," Dr. Colòn said. She looked over at me. "This is something we can fix, Paco. How's that sound?"

"Great," I answered unenthusiastically.

Fixing my problem was not easy. During our next five sessions, we talked about my feelings, my thoughts about my feelings, and my feelings about my feelings. And we spent quite a bit of time discussing JoJo.

Throughout those first three weeks, Dr. Colòn tried to get me to rate my level of anger on a chart she had drawn up. Every time I got mad I was supposed to take the chart out and record data on it. This proved to be easier said than done. The point of the exercise was simple: once I was able to recognize when I was becoming enraged, I could do things to calm myself down before losing control. When I got angry I was to place a check mark next to the level of anger I felt at that moment. I was to use a scale of one to 100. A ten meant I was calm. A ninety meant I was out for blood. The problem was, I never recorded a number higher than twenty. Once I hit thirty, I completely forgot the chart, the pencil, and everything else in my life. After thirty, el fuego took over.

The way this was supposed to work was that I would document my reaction to my own anger. Did I throw something? Did I break something? Did I yell something? Recording this stuff as it happened was supposed to get me to become better at realizing my problem and controlling my response. I just couldn't do it, though. I was too pumped up when I was mad. I couldn't write anything down; I could barely speak!

At the end of three weeks, not only did I feel like I had been beaten up, but I had gotten into two more fights at school. One was a fistfight with a classmate. The other was with the crossing guard.

Dr. Colòn continued being positive, despite my lack of progress. "Paco, I'm proud of you."

"For what?" I asked, sadly. "I'm not getting better. I think I may be getting worse."

She stood up and sat next to me on the couch. "You are trying to dig deep down into yourself and explore what makes you tick. I'm proud of you for that, and I know that you'll get better because of it," Dr. Colòn said. "Still, we're not making as much progress as I had hoped we would. I think we need to change our thinking a bit."

Dr. Colòn stood up and looked at me strangely, "Not every kid with a killer instinct needs what I think you do."

I was listening. I wondered what she had in store for me next.

"Every time you get mad, I've been telling you to record your feelings. The problem is that you can't record them, because you're too mad. That isn't getting us where we need to be. We need to get rid of that energy—the energy that makes you explode. This energy is making it impossible for you to pick up that pencil to write down your feelings." She paused. "So here's what I'm thinking: you should buy a punching bag."

"What?" I asked. Had Dr. Colòn gone crazy? "A punching bag?"

"Yup." She smiled. "I want you to hang it up in your apartment, and when you feel angry about something, I want you to punch it," she said. "How does that sound?"

"Honestly, it sounds pretty crazy." I laughed. "But I guess I could try it. It's better than punching someone's head in, right? What's the catch?"

"There's no catch, Paco," she said. "I'm trying to find a way to help you turn down the flame on el fuego and place your killer instinct on the back burner. Maybe this will work. I think the chart was probably not the best idea for you."

"So, you're saying that I actually hit something when I'm mad?"

"Well," she paused again, "yes. I recommend it. I think it will be an interesting experiment. The real hard work comes after that, when we start talking about you visiting JoJo. I think it could really help you."

My heart started to race at the thought of seeing my brother. "Let's just try the punching bag first."

CHAPTER FIVE

EL BUHO

The first thing I remember about the gym was the smell. It was bad. The combination of sweat and deodorant made me nauseous. But I wasn't going to be there long. All I wanted to do was see if I could purchase a used punching bag.

Not having enough money to buy a new one, my father gave me what little extra he had and told me to head over to the Rock River Police Athletic League Boxing Club. Situated between an auto body repair shop and a lumberyard on Railroad Avenue, the Rock River PAL was a tiny, concrete structure that used to house a mom-and-pop printing company. The presses had been moved out in favor of a boxing ring. Surrounding the ring were several punching bags, big and small, that hung from the low ceiling by metal chains.

After I had gotten past the smell of the gym, I started to focus on the sounds. The roar of a passing freight train combined with the music from several different boom boxes was an interesting combination of violent shakes, piercing whistles, and loud salsa and hip-hop beats.

Standing inside the door of the gym, I looked around. On the walls were fight posters that the Police Athletic League must have spent quite a bit of time and effort obtaining. Some of them looked pretty old. Not that I would have recognized the fighters' names anyway. Although I would catch an occasional fight with my dad on television, I didn't follow boxing. I didn't really follow any sport—aside from an occasional Phillies game. It's probably because my one year of youth baseball was cut short when I was kicked off for fighting. The same thing happened to me on the football team.

Standing there waiting for someone to notice me, I watched as several dozen individuals did their thing. Some shadowboxed in front of the mirror. Others jumped rope. A few more hit the various punching bags. I soaked it all in. I had never been in a place like this before.

I watched as a pair of teenagers slugged it out in the gym's lone ring, located in the middle of the room. They didn't move artfully, like the pros did on television. They looked awkward, even mechanical at times. Their motion was neither fluid nor consistent. I remember thinking that not only could I do what they were doing, but I could probably beat the two of them easily.

When the bell rang, indicating that the round was over, I saw the two combatants hug each other. As far as I could tell, they had just spent the last several minutes trying to knock each other out. Why would they hug? They seemed to have some sort of mutual respect for one another, and their display of sportsmanship was unfamiliar to me. I didn't understand it.

Just then, a Hispanic man in his mid-forties, who sported a thin mustache, came up to me. I stared closely at him as he sized me up. About five feet ten, he was dressed in sneakers and a black nylon sweat suit. He was balding slightly and his nose looked as though it had been broken, perhaps more than once. He had a stopwatch hanging around his neck and a towel draped over his shoulder. He wasn't big, but he was rock hard. It didn't look like he had an ounce of fat on him. There was no question that he belonged in a place like this. As a matter of fact, he looked like he could beat up the two boxers who just finished sparring, as well as everyone else in the gym.

"Que pasa, amigo?" he said. "Can I help you with something?"

"Yea," I said. "I'm here to buy a punching bag."

"Is that so?" responded the man. "This isn't a sporting goods store, chico."

"I know that," I said abrasively. "Don't you have a beat-up bag that you don't want anymore?"

"All our bags are beat up," answered the man dryly. "That's the way they're supposed to be. People come in here to hit them."

I remember thinking how much of a wise guy he was, and how his sarcastic comments sounded like things I would say. But I didn't admire him for it. I disliked him for putting me off. I muttered something under my breath before turning to leave.

"Did you say something?" he asked, taking a step toward me.

"Not to you," I responded rudely.

The man's lips curled into a small smile. I couldn't figure out why. He couldn't have appreciated my tone of voice. "I thought

I heard you say something, chico," he said. "But if you tell me you didn't, you didn't." The man crossed his arms in a confident way.

"I didn't," I repeated.

"Say, why do you want to buy a used punching bag anyway?" the man asked.

"What do you care?" I said. "You're not going to sell me one."

"Es verdad. That's true," said the man. "I was just curious. But if you're afraid to tell me, that's alright."

"I'm not afraid, man," I said, starting to get angry, wondering why this guy seemed to be provoking me. "You want to know why?" I said. "I want a bag so I can hit it rather than the side of someone's face."

I said what I did simply for shock value, but in many ways, it was the truth. Hearing it come out of my mouth, though, made me raise an eyebrow as I realized how vicious it sounded. I expected a similar response from the man, only he didn't seem at all fazed. He stood there, holding on to both ends of the towel as he pulled it tightly against the back of his neck.

I looked at him for what seemed like an eternity, waiting for him to say something. But he just stood there, looking at me. When it appeared that he wasn't going to respond, I turned once again to leave.

"You a tough guy?" he asked.

I turned back around yet again. "Tough enough," I said, starting to sense that el fuego wanted to make an appearance before the day was through. Before I knew it, my hands, though still at my side, had balled into fists.

"Then why don't you join the gym, tough guy?" asked the

man, obviously noticing my change in posture. "You can hit your punching bag here."

"I don't want to join this stinkin' gym," I said. I had tried sports before, and it didn't take me long to realize that I wasn't a joiner.

"Well, as you can see, we've got speed bags for hand-eye coordination, double-end bags for practicing defense, and heavy bags for punching," the man said, pointing to the various bags that were hanging strategically around the gym. "If you're really looking to hit something, I recommend the heavy bag," he said.

"I'm not joining your gym," I said. "If you don't have a bag to sell to me, then I'm done here."

"I'll tell you what, hothead," the man said, the tone of his voice becoming somewhat authoritative. He inched closer to me. My eyes came up to his chest, which, despite being hidden behind a sweatshirt, was well chiseled. "My name is Felix Castillo. I'm the head trainer and manager here at the PAL," he said. "You come here and paint that wall over there and I'll give you a heavy bag. No charge. Think you can handle that, tough guy?"

I looked over at the wall he was referring to. It was in need of a fresh coat of paint. A couple of days after school, helping this guy, and I'd have a heavy bag of my own. I knew my dad, much less Dr. Colòn, wasn't going to let up until I did something. Maybe hitting a bag was just the medicine I needed.

Despite the fact that I didn't like Mr. Castillo one bit, it seemed like a fair enough deal. I unclamped my fists. "Okay, señor," I said. "You got it."

"Muy bien," he said. "What's your name?"

"Paco Diaz," I answered.

"Be here tomorrow at four o'clock, Diaz," said Felix Castillo. "And be on time."

Señor Castillo was waiting for me the following day with a paint brush, several buckets of paint and a drop cloth. "You're late," he said.

I looked up at the clock on the wall. It read three minutes past the hour. "It's only a few minutes after four," I said.

"Like I said, you're late," Mr. Castillo said. "Here's everything you need, except a ladder. You'll find one in the storage closet over there.

"Have fun."

I watched as Felix Castillo climbed into the ring to demonstrate some moves to the two boxers who had been sparring. He saw me out of the corner of his eye. "Hey, Diaz!" he shouted. "You here to watch boxing or paint my wall?"

I turned back to my task at hand, once more muttering to myself how much of a jerk this Felix Castillo was.

I was back at the PAL the next day and the day after that. Although I worked hard all three afternoons, I did catch myself watching everything that was going on around me. One afternoon, it was a heavyweight hitting the bag with such ferocity and power, it was intimidating. It was also really cool to watch. The next day, it was a group of middleweights shadowboxing with such intensity that they resembled the two young kids actually fighting in the ring.

It was hard to concentrate in that environment, painting in the middle of such controlled chaos. As I dipped my brush into the bucket of pale gray paint, I realized that I was witnessing, up close and personal, something that not too many people get to see. All I had known about boxing up until that point was what everyone else views when they turn on the television to watch the championship bout, "Live from Las Vegas." It's all very colorful, with the participants and the paying guests looking their best, especially the celebrities who show up to be seen at ringside.

What I was experiencing here in the gym was the opposite. This was the side of boxing the public rarely sees. I was witnessing the grit and the grime associated with a bunch of dreamers. Each of these wannabees thought that if they sweated it out in the gym, went over moves time and again, and pushed themselves to the limit, one day they'd be able to fight under those lights.

In the PAL gym, the only things colorful were the characters who inhabited it. The gym was small, crowded, and windowless. Even the men's room had no view of the world outside. Simply put, this place was not very appealing. In fact, it was a dump. It was a different world, all right, and one I didn't necessarily want to be a part of. Besides, my work was done. It was time to go.

After putting the finishing touches on my masterpiece, I spotted El Buho, which is Spanish for "The Owl." It's what I heard a few of the boxers call Castillo. At the moment, he was shouting instructions in Spanish from alongside the ring. "La derecha, la derecha," he yelled. "Throw the right."

I approached Castillo from behind, interrupting him. "I finished the job," I said. "Now, which bag is mine?"

The PAL manager turned to face me. It was obvious he wasn't exactly thrilled about my rudely disrupting his training session. "You're not done yet," he said, turning back around to watch the action in the ring.

"What do you mean?" I answered. "I just finished."

"Two coats?" he said, still leaning on the ring apron and watching the sparring session.

"You never said anything about two coats?" I answered, my blood starting to boil. I was convinced this guy was doing everything he could to set me off. On the other hand, I was doing everything I could to remain calm. Unfortunately, thinking about Dr. Colón and everything we talked about was not helping.

"Everybody knows a wall needs two coats," said El Buho.

Once again, I felt my hands turn into fists. Señor Castillo must have sensed it, because he immediately turned around.

"Two coats, Diaz, or no bag," he yelled. "That's the deal."

I felt like hitting him. I think he knew it, too. Right then and there, I knew that el fuego had been lit. At least I had enough sense to walk away, back toward the wall. But I wasn't okay. Not yet. Passing by one of the gym's heavy bags that hung quite low, I took a swing, nailing it with a right hand. Although it didn't move all that much, the sound my fist made hitting it was loud. It was a good sound, and I wanted to hear it again. And again.

Next thing I knew, I was flailing away on that bag, firing lefts and rights until my knuckles were raw. The feeling I got when I hit that bag was something I will never forget—all the energy in my body had been released, and I honestly felt at peace. Either that, or I was simply too exhausted to be angry. Stopping and dropping my hands to my side, I stood there huffing and puffing. I glanced over my shoulder and noticed that El Buho was staring at me.

"Not bad," he said, "you're really fast, chico. But you're doing it all wrong."

I was too tired to tell him to go stuff it. Besides, el fuego seemed to have been doused.

"Hands hurt a little, don't they?" El Buho asked.

Boy, did they ever. But I wasn't about to tell *him* that. I looked back at him blankly.

"I have an idea, Diaz," he said, walking over to me. "How would you like to learn how to box?"

"I know how to fight," I said between wheezes.

"I didn't say fight. Fighting is an entirely different activity. I asked if you'd like to learn how to box."

I wasn't quick enough to ask him why. I just figured he didn't like the way I was punching the bag and wanted to let me know I wasn't anything special. "No," I said, thinking that I would have to be crazy to come here and put up with The Owl on a regular basis.

"That's too bad," Castillo said. I thought our conversation would end right there, but he wasn't giving up yet. "I'll tell you what—I'll give you a choice."

"What choice?" I responded.

"You finish the second coat and, like we agreed on, you take one of these bags home," he said. "That will give you something to bang away at when you're mad. Now, that's okay. But you start hitting that thing the wrong way and you could do serious damage to your hands. I've seen it happen a million times."

"Is that right?" I asked, suddenly more interested in the sport he was so obviously selling.

"Your other choice, which is the one I recommend you take, is that you come here and do the same thing—the right way. In the process, you'll learn how to box. It's up to you," he concluded.

I thought for a second. I had participated in a lot of activities in my life and none of them gave me satisfaction. Why would this be any different? Then I looked over at that punching bag again. The truth was, I loved hitting that bag. The rush I got as I unleashed punch after punch was unmatched. I wanted more. But I didn't like the idea of injuring myself because I wasn't punching correctly. Not only my knuckles—but my wrists—felt the sting from hitting the bag for only a few minutes. Even my right shoulder ached.

Until I got el fuego under control, I assumed I was probably going to need a pair of fists that were in perfect working order. Even more pressing was my need to do something to get my dad and Dr. Colòn off my back. "All right, Señor Castillo," I said. "I'll come to the gym for a few lessons."

"Good," he said. "But first you have to apply that second coat."

CHAPTER SIX

FIRE DOWN BELOW

My dad had been a good athlete in his day. He was a scrappy second baseman on his high school baseball team back home in Mayaguez. He was good enough to be invited to try out with the Mayaguez Indians, winners of fifteen Puerto Rican League championships and a pair of Caribbean World Series titles. So I guess I had some athletic genes in my body.

According to my dad, this boxing experiment was a worthwhile one. He talked to me about the attributes I would learn through boxing—discipline, hard work, dedication, and self-control. He said that learning how to box thanks to a fellow Puerto Rican and former amateur champ would be icing on the cake.

My mom wasn't quite so sure. She thought that boxing was the most primitive and brutal of sports. Boxing was the only sport she knew of in which the objective was to cause injury. How was this going to help me learn to be less violent? Mom didn't see it. It was the only organized activity outside of war, she said, in which anger was accommodated. Mom made a very compelling argument against my participation in the sport. Everything she said made sense.

Truthfully, Dr. Colòn wasn't excited about the prospect of my learning how to box either. During our next session, she told me some of her concerns. I'm not sure why, but I felt compelled to defend the sport I barely knew anything about. I spoke to Dr. Colòn calmly, but with passion behind my words. "The guy at the gym says boxing and fighting aren't the same. He says that boxing is a sport, and that it's all about self-control, which is just what you and I were talking about—my learning to control myself. I can't pretend I don't have the killer instinct, I have to deal with it, right?"

"I don't know, Paco," said Dr. Colòn. "I wanted you to find a release for your anger instead of fighting, not engage in more fighting." She chewed on her fingernail, deep in thought. Then she continued. "I just don't know if being surrounded by violence on a daily basis is good for you. I'm not going to say you can't do it, though," she said. "Not yet at least."

It was Thursday and a school holiday. I finished painting that second coat the day before. My dad had taken off from work so he could accompany me to the PAL for my first workout. On the drive over, I thought about what El Buho had said about the difference between fighting and boxing. This was the message I passed along to Dr. Colòn, but I wasn't sure if I actually believed it myself.

I also wondered if I would be a successful boxer. I have to admit, I was pretty nervous about performing well. Sure, I had done a lot of fighting in my twelve years. As a result, I had gotten pretty good. But if Coach Castillo was right and fighting wasn't like boxing, then would I be any good at it? The fighting I had engaged in, which did involve some punching, didn't have any rules. I would kick, pull hair, and bite my adversary—whatever it took. And once I got started, and el fuego kicked in, I couldn't stop. I assumed the sport of boxing had a bunch of rules. Not only did I have to follow them, but I had to do so while I was fighting. I could see how this would be difficult: I would have to control myself during the peak of el fuego's fury. This test, as Dr. Colòn called it, was going to be interesting.

"Diaz!" El Buho shouted as my father and I walked through the front door of the gym. "What are you waiting for?" He pointed to the door to my left. "Go on in the bathroom and get changed."

Trotting off toward the men's room with my gym bag, I looked back to see him shaking hands with my dad. I wondered, with the two of them on the same page, whether this boxing thing might just turn out to be more of Dad's tough love. There was no way I wanted to sign up for a second helping of that. I received my fill at home already. I knew they would talk about me while I was inside the bathroom getting changed.

"Señor Diaz, mucho gusto."

"Coach Castillo, the pleasure is mine."

El Buho smiled. "Your son has a fire in his belly, no?" he spoke rhetorically, knowing the answer to his question.

"Si, only it's in his head, too, and it clouds his judgment." Dad always told me these exact words.

"I think coming here will be a good thing for him, don't you?"

"I wouldn't be here if I didn't."

I changed as quickly as I could. I didn't want to give my

father and El Buho too much time together. One thing I could be thankful for was having spent those days painting the wall at the Rock River PAL. As a result, I was already somewhat used to the stench of the gym. After I had spent only five minutes in the disgusting men's room, the smell settled into my nostrils. Being there became a bit more bearable after that.

Exiting the men's room, I looked over to see if El Buho was still with my dad. He wasn't. I spotted him in the doorway of the one small room that was off to the side of the ring. I figured it was his office. He was busy talking to a young boxer.

The kid was dressed in blue and gold trunks, a gold tank top, and brilliant white boxing shoes. I glanced down at my faded blue t-shirt, tattered gray gym shorts, and high-top canvas sneakers. The sneaks were my dad's, which he wore when doing work around the apartment. Once black, they were now speckled with white spots, from painting the kitchen last summer. They fit, more or less, with two pairs of socks. They were certainly better than my everyday sneakers, which were held together with duct tape. According to my father, his shoes would at least give me some kind of ankle support.

When I asked for a pair of boxing shoes as I was getting my stuff together at home, my dad scoffed. He then looked at me sternly. "Let's see if you stick it out, first, before I run off and buy you shoes." Although the words were hardly a vote of confidence, they made sense. I didn't yet know what to make of boxing, or whether the sport could help me with el fuego and my killer instinct. Not to mention the fact that I had been thrown off every team I'd ever played on and had quit almost everything I'd ever tried. I knew Dad thought that this wouldn't be any different.

Checking out the rest of the gym, I saw boxers of all shapes and sizes. They were sparring, shadowboxing, hitting the bags, and jumping rope. There were about thirty boxers in all crammed into the Rock River PAL Boxing Club that afternoon at two o'clock.

At least I wasn't the only kid in the place. In fact, there were several boxers who were even younger than me. Two were in the ring sparring. Spanish was the predominant language you heard above the loud grunts and growls. The two trainers watching the pair in the ring were the loudest. The boxers, for the most part, did exactly what their coach told them to do, despite being constantly screamed at. I found that to be quite puzzling.

Just then, the sight of Felix Castillo heading my way interrupted my thoughts. "Diaz!" he shouted, brushing past my dad without acknowledging him. "Come over here."

As I started to make my way toward him, I glanced over at my dad. He just looked at me and smiled, like he knew something I didn't. Then he turned and left. I was on my own.

About thirty minutes later, I was sweating and groaning my way through a third set of twenty sit-ups. According to Felix Castillo, my job was simple: I was to do everything he told me to, without exception, without asking any questions, and without expressing any displeasure. Just do it. Those were the rules of our contract, an unwritten pact that was bound the minute I agreed to be trained by him. In return, he would teach me how to box. Obviously, I didn't like the deal. I couldn't recall having signed any working papers.

At first, the physical suffering I was experiencing was almost too much to bear. I didn't feel like I ever got into a rhythm. Yet, the painful burn masked the fact that my muscles were loosening, stretching, elongating. I had never really done much in the way of exercise, so this was new to me. And my exertion felt anything but good, especially when El Buho stood there shouting at me to give him "cinco mas," five more. I began to think that I would rather be home, sitting in my room reading comics or terrorizing my sister, Marisol. Anything but this.

After the sit-ups, it was on to push-ups, and then leg stretches. More than an hour had gone by, and despite my hands being taped, I hadn't even laced on a pair of gloves. I was in pain, and I was sick and tired of hearing Coach Castillo bark at me, "Push it, Diaz! Push it! C'mon, now!"

All the while, El Buho kept telling me to focus on my breathing, which he said was necessary in order to build stamina and endurance. I didn't know what he was talking about.

A few more minutes and he told me to stand up and watch him closely. I was beginning to see red. I could sense el fuego starting to smolder. As El Buho proceeded to show me how he wanted me to skip rope, on one foot at a time—left foot, right foot, left foot, right—I stood there and seethed.

Then, when he threw the rope to me and told me to get to it, I broke our pact. It happened somewhere between recognizing that I didn't have the energy to jump rope, and realizing that I would not get to hit anyone or anything that night. I dropped the jump rope, officially signaling the end to my workout.

"I didn't call time!" yelled Coach Castillo.

"That's okay," I said. "I did."

"You don't get to do that," said El Buho, the anger in his voice reverberating around the gym. "That's my job! Your job is to do what I say!"

"Save it for one of these other guys," I said turning to walk away. As I did, I remember thinking that Dr. Colòn would be happy to learn I had no intention of returning to the Rock River PAL. My father, on the other hand, would be mad—really mad. I was suddenly happy he hadn't bought me those shoes. I wanted out.

Just then, as El Buho yelled at me to stop, one of the other boxers walked toward me. He was a few years older than I was and I had never seen him before. He came right up to me. As I turned to face him, wondering who he was and what he wanted, he started yelling. "You know that teacher you bit in the playground, you punk?" he shouted, pushing me backwards. "That was my grandfather. Let's go outside so I can teach you what it feels like to be attacked."

It didn't matter that I knew I was wrong to have bitten Mr. Bermudez back in October. And, though I know I should have admired his grandson for seeking retribution, I didn't care. Looking at this guy, my eyes narrowed. The fury that had already been building inside me suddenly reached such an intense level, it even caught me by surprise—not to mention Coach Castillo and the rest of the boxers and trainers standing nearby.

Before Mr. Bermudez's grandson had a chance to open his mouth again, I was all over him. I remember hitting him with a left hook to the abdomen that took his breath away—a short, fast and direct punch that came, unbeknownst to me, correctly from my side. It was a punch I didn't even know I was capable of throwing effectively. But, it was apparently a textbook shot. I nailed him with four of my knuckles flush against the part of his stomach right below his rib cage.

As he stood there frozen, trying to suck in some air, I noticed that his hands had dropped to his sides. I proceeded to nail him in the face with a straight right hand. By then, Coach Castillo had caught up to me. He wrapped his arms around my chest and pulled me off. Several others were over the hapless victim, who had slumped to the ground. They were helping him to his feet. He started yelling and cursing, while I tried to get at him through the arms of several trainers and El Buho. I was enraged, lost somewhere between reality and my own warped sense of justice. I was intent on inflicting more pain and damage—even though, somewhere deep down, I didn't want to. I was kicking and flailing away, making it hard for Coach Castillo to contain me. I was in that place again, where the world started and ended, where el fuego blazed. And, when I was there, nothing else mattered.

Because he was still in great shape, Coach Castillo was able to subdue me. As I started to calm down, I began thinking that my father was not only going to be mad, he would be crazy. I had definitely just written myself a ticket to military school. After being at the gym only one night, I was already destined to pack up my things and not return.

That's not what happened, though. I was told to wait off to the side. I then watched as Coach Castillo spoke quietly to Señor Bermudez's grandson before returning to stand directly in front of me. Coach Castillo looked mad. His face was flushed red as he spoke, "You want to fight someone, Diaz?" The veins in his neck bulged as he spoke. His eyes conveyed the same degree of anger his tone of voice indicated. "Fight me then, chico."

I stood there staring at the ground, then back up at El Buho, and then back down at the ground again. I didn't know what to do. I certainly didn't want to fight The Owl. "That guy started it," I said nervously. "You saw him challenge me. He pushed me and—"

"We do not fight in this gym unless it's in there," said El Buho, pointing toward the ring. "If you want to fight so badly, then we can do it in there." He sounded serious.

"I'm just a kid," I responded.

"Then it shouldn't take me long," said El Buho, now inches from my face. He tossed me a pair of boxing gloves and stepped between the ropes and into the ring. "Come inside, tough guy. You've been waiting to punch all night." He threw four or five hard punches into the air.

I was speechless. I never met anyone like him before, and I didn't know how to react to his behavior. I certainly didn't want to step into the ring with him. Thankfully, after several seconds, I didn't have to.

"Okay, I see you don't want to fight," he said. "Then dig this, and dig it good." He removed his boxing gloves and tossed them aside. "You don't change your attitude, chico, you're going to end up behind bars, or worse."

"So what if I do," I said. "I can handle it."

"You think doing time is easy?" El Buho asked. He was shouting now. "You think it's no big deal? You think you're so tough you could handle it? You don't know anything, chico."

"I know enough," I said.

El Buho turned his head away from me. "Henry," he said to one of the other trainers, another Puerto Rican. "I have to leave for a while. You're in charge." Henry nodded, as did several other trainers and boxers. A few of them smirked as well.

"You'll be gone a couple of hours, right?"

"Si," said El Buho. "No mas."

And that's when he took me on a road trip.

CHAPTER SEVEN

THERAPY

Before I knew it, El Buho had dragged me outside and dumped me into the front seat of his pickup truck. After making me strap on my seatbelt, I watched him on the sidewalk as he talked on his cell phone. Then, he got in and started the engine.

"This is kidnapping," I said to him as he pulled away from the curb outside the PAL.

"So sue me," Coach Castillo said, looking straight ahead.

This guy was something else, I thought, as I looked out the window. The leaves had changed. Autumn was in full bloom. I certainly didn't know what to say to El Buho, nor was I particularly interested in having a conversation with him. So, watching the scenery was fine with me. I did wonder where we were headed, however.

After about a half hour, we arrived at our destination: the State Correctional Institution at Graterford, thirty miles west of Philly. I knew right away that I was going to be taught a lesson.

The jail, Pennsylvania's largest maximum-security prison,

was imposing from a distance. Looking up at it from just outside the front gate was downright terrifying.

Everywhere you looked, there were bars. There were bars on the windows, bars on the doors, bars on the bars. In addition to the bars were coiled razor wire, steel security doors, and metal detectors. They didn't call it maximum security for nothing.

"Let's go, Diaz," said El Buho. "I want you to meet someone."

My heart began racing. What Coach Castillo didn't know, and what I had been thinking about ever since I saw the outline of the prison on the horizon, was that JoJo, my brother, whom I hadn't seen in four years, was here. He had been transferred to Graterford on his eighteenth birthday and had been here ever since. We got a letter a few years back and I remembered hearing Mom and Dad talking about it. But how could El Buho know that, I wondered. Did he know that? Was he going to introduce me to my own brother? A thousand other questions bombarded my brain as a brawny black corrections officer approached the truck.

"El Buho Castillo!" the guard called out. "Que pasa, mi amigo?"

"Billy Reed!" said Coach Castillo. "Thanks for seeing me on such short notice."

The two men shook hands through the open window on the driver's side of El Buho's truck.

Whew, I remember saying to myself. I guess Coach didn't know JoJo was here at Graterford.

"Paco Diaz, this is Bad Billy Reed, one of the best amateur boxers to ever come out of Philly," said El Buho. "And Billy, this is Paco Diaz, a punk kid who just thinks he's bad."

The African-American guard, who looked like he could still go a few rounds himself, smiled. "Time to go to school, son," he said to me with a smirk. I stepped out of the car and followed him. As we walked through the front door and into the prison, I took a whiff. It smelled a little better than the Rock River PAL, but not much. And it definitely wasn't an inviting a place. In fact, everything about it was horrible.

"Ready for a tour?" Billy Reed asked me.

"Do I have a choice?" I asked, as spiteful as ever.

Billy chuckled. "You're right," he said as he turned to El Buho. "This kid does need a lesson."

Ignoring the look of contempt on my face, Bad Billy Reed escorted me through a large metal door.

Passing across the threshold, I turned back to El Buho. "Aren't you coming?" I asked.

"I've seen it before," he responded with a smile.

Our first stop on the tour was Cell Block D. I didn't know what to expect, but by the look on Bad Billy's face as we entered this wing of the prison, I guessed it was going to be an eye-opening experience. We turned the corner into a huge room that seemed longer than a football field. Prison cells, each of them six feet by nine feet, lined both walls, two stories high. We stood at the end of the hallway that ran down the length of the floor. Billy told me the residents called this stretch of concrete Broadway, after the famous street in New York. It was where institutionalized convicts and recently processed arrivals gathered several times a day to be counted, shepherded off to the dining room and given some free time to "hang around."

Billy then whispered to me that one inmate had been knifed

48

by a member of a rival gang in the middle of Broadway earlier that month. I gulped, loudly. "Let's go," Billy said, taking a step down the center aisle, between the cells.

"Where?"

He pointed to the far end of the cell block.

"Down there?" I asked.

"Yup."

"You're kidding, right?" I said nervously. Then I stopped walking. "Listen, I get the point. Prison sucks. Okay, I get it."

"Not yet you don't. Walk with me, son, or you can stay here alone." Billy kept walking. "You don't follow me down this hall, you can't get out of here." Then he pointed at the prisoners. "In fifteen minutes, it's dinner time. Then these doors open up. I wouldn't want to be standing there alone if I were you."

Just as those words escaped his lips, a prisoner screamed, "You can leave him here with me!"

He finished those words and I started walking as fast as I could toward Billy. My entire body was shaking at this point. Once I caught up with Billy, we began to stroll down Broadway. I kept my eyes focused on the far wall, at the end of the room. I didn't want to make eye contact with any of the inmates. I could feel them staring at me from the rafters as well as the ground floor.

"Fresh meat!" one convict yelled.

"Fresh meat!" shouted another.

Within seconds, the entire cell block, all 240 cells and 480 prisoners, were yelling: "Fresh meat." The sound was deafening. Every time I heard another voice scream toward me I flinched.

Several of the convicts spit in my direction. Although I was walking in the middle of the corridor, I wasn't out of harm's way.

Some of the inmates, especially those on the second tier, were accomplished spitters. They were adept at hitting me squarely on the chest, back and side of my head—with pinpoint accuracy.

Although he was walking right next to me, Billy Reed was dry as a bone.

"Arriba, arriba!" one convict yelled, mocking my Hispanic heritage.

"Show me a picture of tu mama!" shouted another. They were saying anything and everything they could to get me to look at them. I refused. The truth was, I was too scared. The end of Broadway seemed like it was in Canada. I didn't know if I could make it all the way there without starting to run.

"Open Number Seventy-two!" yelled Billy to a guard at the opposite end of the room, who was sitting in a small, caged office. After the other officer punched a few keys on his computer, one of the cells opened automatically. Out stepped a hulking, bald, Hispanic inmate in standard prison attire: navy blue hospital scrubs. By cutting off his short sleeves, the con was able to advertise the two colorful tattoos he had on his enormous right arm and the more extensive artwork he displayed on his left. There, the ink covered every inch of his skin from his wrist to his shoulder. Around his neck was a tattoo of barbed wire.

"Inmate Number 48642!" called Billy. "Take a walk on Broadway!"

As the rest of the population on Cell Block D continued to shout vulgar insults, the largest man I had ever seen in my life lumbered up next to me. He neither extended his hand nor spoke. He just walked alongside me, looking straight ahead as well.

"Antonio," said Billy Reed. "Tell this boy about the joint."

The inmate glanced down at me with eyes as dark and as empty as a vampire's. I felt a shiver run down my spine. Then he turned his gaze back to the front. "You've got to mentally prepare yourself for a place like this," he said slowly, making sure I listened to every word he said. It was hard, with all the shouting going on around me, but I heard him loud and clear. "You have to—especially on that first day. They'll strip-search you, hose you down, and give you this outfit to wear for the next ten years or so. Within your first hour, you'll have your life threatened by a bunch of hard dudes, and they mean it, too. Then you'll eat your first prison meal and wish your mommy was there to cook you up some carne asada." Antonio added. "That's just the first day."

As I tried to swallow the lump that was forming in my throat, a rat ran across Broadway directly in front of us. It came from one cell on the right and scampered into the opposite cell on the left. I flinched. As the rat ran, the residents of Cell Block D let out a collective cheer.

"Prison is a stressful place, hermano," said Antonio. "You're getting a gift today, and you don't even know it. This little preview will keep you from being as shocked when you join us for real."

I glanced over at Bad Billy Reed. He was just walking, soaking it all in, like he had never heard it before.

"Once you get here, you can't act out," Antonio went on. "If you do, the guards will label you a troublemaker, and then you'll be subjected to a world of hurt. They can make your life miserable." He looked down at me, directly into my eyes, for the first time. "You're not a troublemaker, are you, boy?" asked Antonio.

I shook my head no. Antonio grunted his disbelief.

"Good, 'cause you want to keep a low profile here. Remember, prison is full of predators. It's wise when you leave your cell to have several inmates go with you—especially to the shower. The problem," Antonio added with a chuckle, "is finding the right ones to ask to come along."

At that point, he stopped. So did Billy. I hadn't realized it, but we had walked the entire length of Broadway. Antonio looked down at me again with those eyes. "Anything else you want to know?"

I again shook my head from side to side. Billy started to push me toward the exit while the other guard came out of the office to usher Antonio back to his cell. "Hey, don't you want to know what I'm in here for?" asked Antonio.

"No," I said, finally able to speak. I quickly let the door close behind me.

Less than an hour later, I had seen enough of prison to know that I didn't want to end up there. I wanted to go home.

"One more stop," said Billy, opening the door to the prison's hospital.

Thus far, I had managed to walk through several cell blocks and rooms without coming across JoJo. I had witnessed three near-fights among inmates, had seen too many facial scars to count, and had watched several more of Graterford's vast assortment of vermin make an appearance. I don't think I breathed the whole time I was there. Not only was I scared of what I was seeing, but I was also terrified about possibly bumping into my brother. I didn't know what I would do if that happened. I didn't know what I would say. I wanted to get out of there before I was forced to dredge up four years of pain and sorrow on the spot.

Once inside the hospital, I looked around. No sign of JoJo.

Just bed after bed of sick inmates, some of them dying, riddled by drugs and disease. Two of the few who could speak told me they couldn't wait until I was incarcerated at Graterford.

I turned to Billy. "Okay, I get the message," I said. "Can I go, please?" I could see he knew I was sincere.

Within minutes, we were back in the lobby. El Buho was there, talking to a couple of officers who seemed to know him well. I wondered if they were ex-boxers, too. As Bad Billy Reed stuck out his hand to me, I shook it. "I hope I never see you here," he said.

He and El Buho hugged before the trainer and I headed for the parking lot. Once in the truck, I breathed a sigh of relief, only El Buho didn't really know why. He thought it was because of what I had just experienced. I rubbed my hands over my eyes repeatedly, opening them after I thought I had wiped away everything I had seen. I glanced over at the prison yard one last time as we began to pull away. That's when I saw him.

JoJo was standing in between two other inmates. He was much bigger than I remembered, and not only because four years had gone by. It was obvious he spent quite a few afternoons in the courtyard lifting weights. I couldn't blame him. The place he lived was the scariest place I could ever imagine. Even though we were about two hundred yards away, I had no doubt about it: that face was my brother's. And I was sure that our eyes met, if ever so briefly, just as El Buho stepped on the accelerator and sped away.

CHAPTER EIGHT

THE VISIT

That night, at home, I couldn't concentrate. Not during dinner, when my dad was asking me about my first day at the gym. Not while I was doing my homework. Not while I was getting ready for bed either. I couldn't stop seeing JoJo in my head. His eyes, his huge frame, the look on his face—it all haunted me. And the fact that he was where he was made it even harder for me to free my mind. I felt terrible for him.

When it was about an hour past my normal bedtime, my parents came into my room, noticing that my light was still on. I sat upright in my bed, staring straight ahead. This was the same room I used to share with JoJo. As I stared at the wall opposite my bed, I remembered a time when JoJo slept right there against that wall. Although his bed had long since been removed, I still imagined him asleep there some nights.

"What's bothering you, Paco?" my mom asked, as she entered my room and placed her hand on my shoulder. "You're not yourself tonight. No dinner. No television."

"Did something happen at the gym?" my dad asked sternly, not moving from his post near the doorway. "Don't tell me you're ready to quit already, because—"

I cut him off before he began to yell. "I'm not quitting. Get off my back."

Just then, Marisol walked into my room, wearing her pajamas and carrying her favorite doll. "Quiero agua," she said in a whiny voice. "I want some water."

"Marisol!" my mother said. "You should be asleep."

As my mom picked up my sister and carried her back to her room, my dad moved closer to my bed, standing over me. "Paco," he said, his voice getting louder, "I expect you to stick with boxing. You made a commitment to Señor Castillo, and I expect you to honor it. Comprende?"

"Si, papa," I answered, although I wasn't thinking about boxing or El Buho. I was thinking about the State Correctional Institution at Graterford. I was thinking about JoJo. But I couldn't tell my father that as he left the room and shut the lights behind him. Although I knew I wasn't going to nod off any time soon, I put my head down on my pillow and closed my eyes. I thought about JoJo, and how we made eye contact just before El Buho's truck pulled away. I wondered if he was thinking about me right now as well. That night, all my dreams were about my brother.

By the time I got dressed the next morning I knew what I had to do. I was ready to do it. The only problem: how would I get back to Graterford?

Walking to school, I came up with a plan. I would enlist the help of Felix Castillo. After all, he was the guy who caused this problem to begin with. All day in school, I couldn't wait for the bell to ring. At three o'clock, I bolted down the front steps of St. Joe's and ran as fast as I could to the Rock River PAL.

Crashing through the front door, I looked up to see El Buho staring at me from inside his office. "I didn't think you'd be back today," he said. "I'm impressed, Diaz."

"I'm not here to train today," I said. "I need a favor."

"You do, huh?" said El Buho. "I didn't know we knew each other well enough to start asking for favors. What can I do for you?"

"Can you drive me back to Graterford this afternoon," I said.

EL Buho looked confused. "Why, chico?"

"I'll tell you on the way."

For the next half hour, I explained to El Buho about my brother, my so-called killer instinct and my psychologist's desire to have me visit him. I told him I hadn't even thought about this meeting seriously until my eyes met with JoJo's the previous afternoon. And I told Coach Castillo that I thought it was his duty to bring me back to Graterford, given that he had brought me there the day before.

The only thing I left out—which I wasn't dying to tell my father either—was how Dr. Colòn didn't want me to box. I also failed to mention that I was unsure if I wanted to continue with boxing myself. While I talked El Buho just drove. He didn't say anything. He didn't pass judgment. He let me talk and he listened. He didn't even say I owed him one for agreeing to drive me to Graterford.

After we arrived, Coach Castillo told me he would go visit

with Billy Reed while I went to see JoJo. As we parted, he wished me good luck. I needed it, because fifteen minutes later, I was sitting in a strange room on an uncomfortable blue plastic chair, behind six inches of sound-proof glass, waiting for my brother to be brought out. As I did, I got pretty sad. The other inmates around me, who were talking to loved ones, looked tired and defeated. Even though I didn't know much about the sport yet, I compared them each to beaten boxers, who have realized in the final round that they have nothing left to fight for. Not even their pride.

My heart pounded inside my chest. I hadn't seen my brother since I was eight years old. I didn't know what to say to him. I wondered if he would look as broken as these other men did. I wondered what he would say to me. Plus, JoJo didn't know that I had come to see him. The only thing the guards told him was that he had a visitor. As a result, I was as unsure about this meeting as anything else in my life up to that point. A thousand thoughts raced through my head, but one kept coming to the forefront: would my brother want to see me?

Just then the door on the far wall opened. Into the reception area walked a burly guard followed by a young Latino—the same Latino I saw on the fence the day before, the same Latino who grew up sleeping five feet away from me. I was dismayed at first when I noticed the sullen expression on JoJo's face, not unlike the rest of the cons I saw talking to their wives, parents, and children. It was quite different from the expressive teenaged face I remembered. Back then, it didn't take much to make him smile and laugh.

He walked over to the chair across from me and sat down. I noticed that he was shaking a bit, and I wondered if he was as nervous as I was. As soon as his eyes met mine, they came alive. So did his mouth. He grinned from ear to ear. I grinned, too. Then he picked up a telephone receiver that was hanging on his side of the glass. He indicated to me with his hands that I should do the same. "Paco," he said, choking up a bit. "It *was* you yesterday in that car. I knew it!"

"Yeah," I said, my eyes starting to fill up with tears.

"Listen to your voice." JoJo closed his eyes. "Man, just the way I remember it."

I smiled, "Yours sounds the same, too."

"Sometimes when I close my eyes at night, I hear that voice. It's good to see you, brother." JoJo rubbed his hands over his eyes, trying hard to contain his tears. A moment later, he was composed again. "So what were you doing here yesterday?" he asked.

"It was like a school trip," I said, lying.

"You weren't going to come see me," he said. "But you changed your mind when we spotted each other."

"Something like that," I said sheepishly. "I guess I was scared."

JoJo removed the receiver from his ear and began tapping it against his forehead. He seemed to be deep in thought. "You're here now."

"Yup, I am," I said.

"Man, you got big," he said, looking me over.

"So did you," I replied.

"Not much else to do in here," he said, flexing his giant right bicep.

Just then—from out of nowhere—I felt el fuego rumble inside of me. "You could have written me a letter or two, JoJo." I spoke with force behind each word.

"I wrote you a hundred," he answered. "But I ripped them all up before mailing them."

"Why?"

"You don't understand what it's like in here, Paco. You start to question yourself. Do I deserve a family? Do I deserve a brother? A lot of times the answer I came up with was no. I'd start to write you and then I'd think that you were better off without a piece of junk like me in your life. I'm so ashamed of what I've done. The truth is, I didn't know how to tell you how sorry I was."

I really didn't know how to respond to this speech. JoJo looked down at his feet for a few moments as I thought about what he had just said.

It seemed like an eternity before I finally did speak. I did everything I could not to cry as I said, "You were my best friend." I put my fist up against the glass that separated JoJo and me.

He put his fist up across from mine and banged on the glass lightly. "Man, why'd it take you so long to come and see me? I've missed you, bro."

"I missed you, too. For a long time I hated you for what you did, JoJo," I said. "I hated you for committing the crime, but I hated you even more for leaving me. Dad would never let me come here either. He doesn't know that I'm here now. We don't even mention your name at home."

JoJo hung his head.

"Seeing you makes me feel better, though, because I still need my brother," I said.

"Good," JoJo said, smiling. "I need my brother, too." Our eyes were locked on one another as we spoke these words. I knew in that moment, that JoJo would always be a part of my future. And to be honest, it was the greatest feeling I had felt in years.

He continued, "I know I messed up my life, Paco. I know I hurt a lot of people. Especially my family. I can't take back what I've done," he said. "I can only tell you that not a day goes by that I don't regret it. I'm paying the price, Paco. I've lost a lot. I don't want to lose you again."

I didn't know what to say. I was still hurt and I was still angry. But I was absent any killer instinct. Actually, I wanted nothing more than to reach out and hug my brother. I knew right away that coming to see him was a great decision. It felt good to know he was alive.

After that, we just sat there a while, alternately looking at each other and then down at our shoes. JoJo broke the silence, "So what have you been up to?"

I answered him right away. "I'm doing some boxing. I mean, I'm just starting, but I like it." As these words escaped from my mouth, I was a little surprised by them. I guess I really did like boxing. "I had my first training session at the Police Athletic League gym last night."

"You're going to be boxer?" JoJo asked.

"I don't know," I said. "I've got some problems with my temper. Mom and Dad are making me see a shrink. I'm only going so Dad doesn't send me to military school," I continued. "I just started this boxing thing, and I don't know if I have what it takes to fight in the ring. I'm not really into sports, you know. And my coach is a real burro."

"Paco, listen to me," said JoJo. "The biggest mistake I made, and the one that led directly to me ending up here, is that I didn't join the PAL, or the football team, or the baseball team. I joined a gang. So, instead of hitting a walk-off home run or scoring the game-winning touchdown, I'm here, in prison," he said. "If you've got anger issues, Paco, all the more reason why you need to stick with something like boxing. I wish I had. You let your anger get the best of you, and you'll end up like me," he added.

I looked up at my brother and felt really bad for him at that moment. I didn't want to end up in prison. I didn't want my anger to control me any longer. In the middle of these thoughts, one of the guards shouted, "Diaz! Time to say goodbye."

"I gotta go, bro," JoJo said. "Thanks for coming. It means everything to me."

"Me, too," I responded.

"Stick with the boxing, Paco," he said, before hanging up. "Then come back real soon and tell me all about it."

On Monday in Dr. Colòn's office, things went pretty well. She was very happy about my progress and it felt good. "You saw your brother?" asked Dr. Colòn in disbelief. "That's wonderful, Paco. But I didn't think you felt ready to do that."

"It kind of just happened," I said.

"I'm proud of you," she said. "I'm surprised, too. Do you feel like talking about it?"

"Believe it or not, Dr. Colòn, I do," I said, grinning. "I also want to tell you that I'm going to give this boxing thing a shot, even though I know you're against it."

"Well, you caught me off guard with your visit to JoJo," she said. "I'm willing to wait and see if you've got any more surprises up your sleeve."

Back at the gym the following afternoon, El Buho told me he would tape my hands in his office rather than out on the floor.

"What gives?" I said to him. "I don't want any special treatment."

"Trust me, Diaz, you won't get any," El Buho said. "I just wanted to tell you something. You know the guy you punched out the other night, Elmer Bermudez?"

"I do now," I said.

"Well, he's waiting for you over by the bathroom," Coach Castillo said. "Go shake his hand, then come right back here."

I walked over to Elmer Bermudez and extended my hand to him, something I couldn't recall ever doing to anyone before, much less someone I had recently pummeled. It was a weird feeling, but not a bad one. He returned the shake. Neither of us spoke nor even looked at each other. But, as far as I was concerned—and I think as far as Elmer was concerned, too—the matter was closed. The fact that I was able to do that made me feel like I was making progress toward taming el fuego. A few weeks ago I would never have agreed to shake hands with someone who I had gotten into a fight with.

When I poked my head back in the office, I saw that Coach Castillo was now sitting behind his desk, beneath a bunch of black and white photos of boxers, most of them former Rock River PAL boys. One picture showed a young Felix El Buho Castillo knocking out his opponent en route to winning the gold medal in the lightweight division of the 1975 National Police Athletic League tournament. "Sit down," said El Buho, offering me the folding chair opposite his desk.

I sat on the edge of the seat, my feet dangling above the

floor.

"Listen, Paco," he began. It was the first time I could recall him addressing me by my first name. "We both know that you've got a fire inside you. I do believe that with some work, it can serve you well in the ring. But if you don't follow my instructions, and learn to box the right way, it could also work against you. It can burn you down, chico."

I nodded.

"Do you realize that Elmer is a seasoned boxer six years older than you, with a lot of experience in the ring?" he asked.

I hadn't, until then. I smiled.

"Throwing a lucky punch every once in a while doesn't make you a boxer," he added, wiping the grin off my face.

"Who says it was lucky?" I shot back.

"I do," said El Buho. "You're out of control, with no technique and certainly no discipline. You bring that stuff into the ring and you'll get beat every time. I don't care how many lucky punches you throw. An experienced boxer will get inside your head and once he's in there, he'll beat you up bad, chico. Real bad."

I made a face, as I only half-believed what he was telling me.

"You're a head case, Diaz. Your pent-up anger and frustration has no place in the ring. That's my first job in training you. I need to teach you discipline. Your entire life is going to change. When we're finished working, and there will be a ton of hard work, you'll be a boxer—someone in total control of his emotions. It's not going to be easy," he added. "So, from this moment forward, you're here to work hard and listen to me. As long as you do, I'll help you become a better person."

I nodded my head in agreement but couldn't help saying, "You and everyone else."

"Well, you've already proven that you can't do it on your own. And that's okay, chico. Most people can't. There's no shame in accepting help." El Buho said.

Then he leaned in closer to me, looking deep into my eyes, "I can help you get rid of those demons inside of you. Believe me, I know all about them."

CHAPTER NINE

GROUND RULES

As I ran next to the train tracks, alongside the rocky river-bed that gave the town its name, I dodged broken bottles and warped railroad ties. I ran as hard and as fast as I could, while concentrating on my breathing. I could feel my leg muscles struggling under the weight of my body. I could also feel my chest pounding. Every part of my body was hurting, all but begging me to stop running—everything except my heart, that is.

Coach Castillo had lectured, explaining in his words, that "road work can be the most boring, most unappealing part of a boxer's training regimen." He also was quick to point out that it was necessary, so that I would have something left in my tank in the later rounds. I heard his voice in my head as I ran as hard and fast as I could. I could tell that I wasn't in the kind of shape I wanted to be in. Not yet at least.

I looked down. My dad's sneakers were holding up okay, so I wasn't too concerned that I would twist an ankle. I was more worried that I'd be late. Coach Castillo told me that if I was late for training more than once, he was through with me. I left my house a few minutes after I had planned on leaving, so I had to make up the time here, along the train tracks.

As part of my training, El Buho had ordered me to run to the gym and back home every day except for Sunday, my day off. There were two Sunday rules that El Buho insisted on. "First, you spend time with your family," Coach Castillo said. "Then, you have your mom make you a steak and some tostones. That's your new routine for every Sunday. Got it?"

"I got it," I had replied, thinking I wasn't in any position to disagree. It's a good thing I liked beef and fried plantains.

I sprinted the last one hundred yards or so of Railroad Avenue, arriving at the gym with two minutes to spare. I quickly went inside and hurried over to where one of Coach Castillo's assistant trainers was busy taping several boxers' hands. After waiting my turn, I sat down on a folding chair.

"Just made it, eh?" asked the elderly trainer, Henry Garcia, not bothering to look up. "Estas cansado? You tired, Diaz?"

"A little," I said. "I'll be okay."

"You're the kid who punched out Elmer Bermudez the other day, right?" asked the man. "The same kid who painted that wall over there?"

"Yeah, that's me," I said.

The man just started chuckling to himself.

"What's so funny?" I asked, getting a little agitated.

"Nada," said Henry. "Private joke. Yup, I heard all about you. You're the crazy one with the killer instinct. I heard you're totally out of control. A head case, no?" he asked in his thick, Spanish accent as he slowly crouched down into a catcher's stance and began taping my hands.

"What do you know about me?" I asked. He was starting to get under my skin.

"Don't worry about what I know," he said. "But just so *you* know, they usually reserve the diagnosis killer instinct for sociopaths. Are you a danger to society? Should I be nervous standing near you?" The man smiled in a sarcastic way, as he continued taping my hands.

"What do you mean?" I snorted, not liking Garcia's tone of voice. I was still stinging a bit from how I had gone from a bad seed to a head case in Coach Castillo's lingo. Plus, I didn't even know who this wrinkled old dude was.

"A killer instinct is used to describe delinquents," Henry said, continuing to tape my hands. "Are you one of those criminales?"

"Why do you care?" I asked, growing more angry with every moment. I could feel that el fuego had become lit. I inched closer to the man. "You scared I might hurt you?" I said with a snarl.

"Scared of you?" responded the seventy-five-year-old trainer, who displayed the telltale marks of having participated in many ring wars during his long life. Surrounding his boxer's nose were two eyebrows of scar tissue and one cauliflower ear. He dropped the tape to look me straight in the eye. "Nah. You're just a punk kid with an attitude problem who got some shrink to make an excuse for him."

That was it. I snapped. Only this time I didn't raise my hands. I chose a less violent, but perhaps more horrific response. I spit in Henry Garcia's face.

It was the same humiliating thing that had been done to me several days before at Graterford Prison. I certainly didn't appreciate it when it happened to me. Now I was acting like one of the convicts. Realizing what I had just done, I stood up, expecting some type of physical retaliation. I was actually surprised when it didn't come. Instead, Henry Garcia reached for the towel that was draped over his shoulder. Then he wiped his face clean and knelt back down. He picked up the tape and looked at me.

Not knowing what to make of this, nor what to do, I sat back down, with a confused look on my face. Having Henry staring at me was uncomfortable. So I did something I don't recall ever doing before. I apologized. "I'm sorry," I said, awkwardly. "I shouldn't have done that. It's just, the things you're saying about me—" I stopped myself.

Henry Garcia crossed me up even further by smiling. I mean, I just spat on this guy who was old enough to be my great-grandfather, and he seemed happy about it! "Muy bien," he said, very good. "You passed the test. You know the difference between right and wrong." He paused to let what he just said sink in. "I was egging you on, Paco. I was trying to get you to explode, and you did. You still have to work on that. But then you apologized. Muy bien. Muy bien. Wait here," he said. "El Buho wants to talk to you. Comprende?"

Coach Castillo, who had apparently been watching the entire scene unfold from his office, came over. I was totally confused when he approached me with a smile. "See? You do realize the difference between right and wrong, chico." Coach Castillo noted, patting Henry on the back as he hobbled past him . Obviously, the old man had performed his task well. "That apology means you're not a social deviant, or a criminal. Not yet at least," he laughed. "The fact that you spit at old Henry in the first place means that you still have trouble controlling your emotions. That, we can work on. I've seen a lot of young kids like you. We can fix you up, Paco. You won't end up in prison if you stick by my side."

"My brother would be happy to hear that," I said.

"And so would your parents, no?"

"Si," I answered.

"Muy bien," said El Buho. "Then, let's get to work."

As I started stretching, I couldn't help but wonder about Felix Castillo. He had no financial interest in helping me, but he seemed intent on doing so anyway. His desire to impose some order on my life and to fix my inner turmoil bordered on an obsession. It was all he could talk about, and we started spending lots of time together. Truthfully, he was helping me more every day. What puzzled me was that I couldn't figure out why he was doing it. Whatever the reason, I decided right then, ten minutes after I spit in Henry Garcia's face, that I would do my best not to let El Buho down.

That day's training was like many other days that followed. I stood punching a heavy bag, first with my left 100 times, and then with my right. Each punch was followed by a shout from El Buho. He either counted the repetition aloud, "one, two, three, four," or he'd scream that something was wrong with my form: "straighten your back, chico" or "move your feet!"

In addition to his loud counting and instruction on the heavy bag, he would be the most vocal as I did my daily 100 push-ups. Even now, if I listen hard enough, I can still hear him screaming at me. "That's ten, eleven, twelve—one more time on twelve, Paco: don't you get lazy in this gym. Get that chest all the way to the floor!

Okay, now *that's* twelve. Thirteen, fourteen, fifteen, sixteen. All the way down, all the way up. We've got a lot more work to do, chico. Twenty-five, twenty-six, twenty-seven. Before we let you into that ring, you need to be as solid as a rock." Then he would slap me hard on my stomach or my back. "Good. Feels strong. You're getting closer. Thirty-eight, thirty-nine, forty. I'm gonna teach you how to box and a lot of other things, Paco. Forty-one, forty-two, forty-three. You have to want it bad, though. You have to want it more than everybody else. Forty-eight, forty-nine. You know that somebody else is training right now. Can you hear him, Paco? Listen. He's doing push-ups in some other gym right at this moment. Are you going to be ready for him? Fifty-six, fifty-seven, fifty-eight. Hit the ground with your chest, Diaz! Earn it! Give me everything you have!"

Sometimes he would get in my face near the end of a set of push-ups. He would kneel down on the ground so that his mouth was inches from my ear. "You want to quit? Seventy, seventy-one. Are you finished? Is that really all you have? Or do you have something more inside you? Is there something deeper?" Hearing his words, I would dig. I would dig deeper then I ever thought I could. "Ninety-nine, one hundred. That's the way." I became stronger and quicker every single day I spent in that gym. And I wouldn't quit—not when I reached 100, not until I couldn't lift myself off the floor. "One-hundred-and-one, one-hundred-and-two. I love it, Diaz! Don't stop now. Don't stop! One-hundred-and-fifteen, one-hundred-and-sixteen . . ."

When I had finally finished the day's workout, Coach would sit me down and tell me how much work we still had left to do. He ended all of our sessions the same way, with a short speech. "That

was a good workout. I know you can do even better, though."
Then he would pat me on the back. I would leave the gym and he
would always stop me. It was as if he always felt the need to remind me that el fuego was still inside me. "Remember to keep your
head on straight. Don't let anybody to get to you. You're in control,
chico. If I hear bad reports, off to military school for you. Do you
understand?"

"Si, yo entiendo." I always answered him the same way—
yes, I understand.

"We've got a long way to go, Paco," El Buho would add.
"But we're getting there."

CHAPTER TEN

OUT OF CONTROL

I had learned early on in my boxing education that motion relieves tension. So I kept shadowboxing as my opponent climbed through the ropes. It was my first amateur fight—a three-rounder—and the first time the outcome would be documented. That is, from tonight on my record would actually be recorded. Nearly a full year had passed since I first began showing up at the Rock River PAL. Now, twelve months later, I was ready to prove myself against an opponent.

Over the past year, I had been in class. It was "Boxing 101"and my professor, El Buho, started me off with the basics. We first worked on my stance—standing with my feet shoulder width apart, angling my toes toward twelve o'clock and two o'clock. Then, he taught me how to correctly throw punches: jabs, hooks, uppercuts and straight right hands. I never knew that so much went into punching, or that technique was so key to effectiveness.

I practiced over and over again. I concentrated on shifting

my weight, extending my arms, keeping my elbow flexed, snapping my wrist, pivoting my feet, rotating my hips, and anchoring my punches by contracting my back muscles. It was a lot to remember, which is why it took such a long time to prepare for my first fight.

In that time, I had also learned how to effectively hit the speed bag, which had been the most frustrating part of my early workouts. It took me a long time to master the rhythm of hitting the bag just the right way so it came off the backboard correctly—so that I could hit it with either a backhand or a straight punch. Eventually I got it. Dad even put up a speedbag in my bedroom, so that I could practice at home for a few minutes every morning. It definitely helped me gain quickness, and I felt great that Dad was taking such an interest in my life.

I spent lots of time dodging blows by bobbing and weaving or slipping and ducking. A good boxer has to make split-second decisions as to which method to use in effectively dodging punches. Every type of punch requires a different dodging technique. Although I hadn't perfected my defense yet, I was certainly getting better. The hardest part for me was remembering to keep my hands up and my head moving at all times. I was constantly reminded that my goal was to be a moving target for my opponent.

Between his speeches and demonstrations, El Buho taught me how to self-condition my body to endure the rigors of the sport. We trained hard, keeping in mind strength, stamina and speed. Once my punching form had received his blessing, about six months after I started, he gave me permission to climb the steps into the ring. Once there, he had me spar with bigger, older, and more seasoned amateurs. I was making progress, though occasionally I would lose my cool. When that happened, I lost my form and my poise, and became a very poor boxer who had a difficult time landing punches. I also broke the rules when I got mad—I knew that outbursts like that during a fight would certainly mean disqualifications.

For the most part, though, I had been able to keep the killer instinct in check. I hoped that I would be able to control el fuego during a real fight as well as I had when sparring.

The ring was proving to be a great place for me to expend my excess energy. As a result, I didn't have much more of it come the following morning. El fuego would still often start up, but it spread only rarely. I was getting good grades and, except for a few minor outbursts, was keeping out of trouble at St. Joe's. Principal Grace was thrilled with my progress, pointing to me as a success story.

I visited JoJo often, with El Buho taking the time to drive me there. My dad never knew; he was just happy that my new-found sport was keeping me in line. Mom, though, went with me to see JoJo a few times. After I confided in her that I had gone against my father's wishes and visited him, she couldn't help but do the same. Seeing her with my brother made me so happy. I'm sure it made JoJo happy, too.

My brother was my biggest fan. He wanted to know everything about my training triumphs and tribulations, down to the tiniest detail. He wanted to know what El Buho was like, what the gym was like, and what lacing up a pair of gloves was like. He was living through me, and my weekly visits to Graterford were the highlight of his life. He only wished that he could be ringside to see me fight himself. "Soon enough," I would tell him, as he inched closer and closer to his first parole hearing.

Even Dr. Colòn had become a believer, thanks to my progress. She became somewhat of a fan, too, dropping by the gym every now and then to watch me do my thing. She shared with me a quote that she'd researched from a writer named George Garrett, who used to be an amateur boxer. The quote really touched to the heart of my situation so I kept it in my locker at the gym. Garrett had written:

"Many good and experienced fighters, as has often been noted, became gentle and kind people. . . . They have the habit of leaving all their fight in the ring. And there, in the ring, it is dangerous to invoke too much anger. It can be a stimulant, but is very expensive of energy. It is impractical to get mad most of the time."

Now, as I thought about that quote, I stared across the ring at David Godwin, a fifteen-year-old veteran of ten amateur bouts, all of which he had won. He had emigrated from the Bahamas a few years earlier and was now living in nearby Easton, home of former heavyweight champion of the world Larry Holmes. In his short time in the States, and in the ring, Godwin had built a reputation as a hard-nosed brawler with a big right hand.

I was no longer lanky, having put on some bulk after twelve straight months in the gym. I now weighed a solid 112 pounds and was fighting as a flyweight. But, on catching the eye of Godwin as we waited for the referee's instructions, I didn't feel so strong and fit. I felt nervous.

This wasn't a feeling I was accustomed to and I didn't like it. I hoped that once the bell rang, the knots in my stomach would go away. They did. Only it wasn't because I calmed down. It was because thirty seconds into the fight David Godwin tagged me with a right hook that left me, literally, seeing stars.

The fact that my chin hurt made me forget about my midsection. It also made me mad. So much so that I disregarded just about everything Coach Castillo had taught me and threw caution to the wind. After being hit with another right hand, I unleashed my entire arsenal on Godwin. In the remaining minute-and-a-half of the round I threw every punch I could think of: uppercuts, right hooks, left hooks, jabs, and body shots. But I was throwing them so wildly that none of them were landing. I was trying to fight David, not box him. Sure enough, the experienced boxer dodged every blow. And when the bell rang, he was standing there smiling. I was completely spent and he knew it

Returning to my corner, I knew I had let my emotions get the best of me. I had forgotten why Coach Castillo had me do all that road work. I had also dismissed his mandate to do exactly what he said. In short, I had broken our contract and let El Buho down. I was so angry that I felt just about ready to quit.

"Ready to quit?" he asked as I sat down on the stool between rounds.

"Are you serious?" I replied between gasps. I allowed my mouthpiece to dangle from my lips so I could get some air into my lungs.

"Are you?" he answered back.

I didn't think I could lift my arms for another ten seconds, much less four minutes. But I figured there was really only one answer to that question. "No," I responded.

"Muy bien," he answered. "Then, let's get back to the game plan."

As Coach Castillo reminded me that my job was to stick and move, keeping David Godwin off balance while looking for an opportunity to hit him with a right hand of my own, I glanced over to ringside. There, sitting next to my dad, was Dr. Colòn. I guess she wanted to see if the experiment was working.

It was my first real test and, at the moment, I was in danger of failing. Henry Garcia squeezed a sponge full of water over my head as Coach Castillo stuck my mouthpiece back in my mouth. I stood up so Henry could straighten my headgear while El Buho gave me one last piece of advice before I ventured out for Round Two. "Don't quit. I don't train quitters," he said.

Ding!

I shuffled forward, trying to conserve whatever energy I had left in my attempt to get Godwin to make a mistake. Even if I did get him to commit himself, I didn't know if I had enough in my whole body, much less my right hand, to cause him any concern. Godwin still had plenty left, which he displayed by rushing toward me. He wanted to pick up where he left off. His goal was to frustrate me to the point where I'd tire myself out with another punching frenzy. Either that, or he'd hit me a few more times on the button.

As he came straight at me, I tried to sidestep and hit him at the same time. I didn't move fast enough, though. As I missed with a wild left hook, he nailed me with a right just south of my belt line. A bit too far south. It was an illegal low blow, and the ref saw it. He indicated to Godwin that he was officially warned, and sent him to a neutral corner.

Although that was all well and good, the foul was the worst thing that could have happened. It wasn't just because it knocked the wind out of me. It also caused me to lose my perspective, and with it, my head. In the next minute or so, I went nuts. Just as I had in the previous round, only worse this time, I unloaded on David

Godwin. Gone was any semblance of my game plan, my composure, and my sense of what was fair inside the squared circle. Gone also was my knowledge of boxing and with it the knowledge that El Buho, my father, and my psychologist were all in attendance, hoping to see my progress played out on a grand stage.

I began hitting Godwin with everything I brought with me that night: my fists, my elbows, my knees, you name it. When it seemed like I couldn't possibly take things further, I did. It didn't matter that both his corner men and El Buho were already rushing into the ring. As Godwin slumped against the corner post, stinging from a knee to the groin, I head-butted him through the ropes. My final act, and the worst decision I made that night, was the punch I threw at the ref, who at that point was trying to wrestle me to the canvas. It was the only punch I threw all night that landed.

As I was being led out of the ring to chorus of boos from the crowd, I perused the seats at ringside. I saw that my cheering section wasn't applauding. From the look on the faces of my dad and Dr. Colòn, it was clear that they had nothing to celebrate.

CHAPTER ELEVEN

DANCING

When I walked back into the locker room after the fight, I felt awful. I couldn't believe what happened out there. It had been so long since I had acted that way. I was embarrassed. More than anything, though, I was disappointed in myself. Deep down, I knew I could be a great boxer. All I had to do was stay in control, but I simply couldn't seem to do that. Frustrated and exhausted, I slumped down into the corner of the room and rested my swollen face in my hands.

When El Buho walked into the room a moment later, I could tell that he was angry at me. After all, I had completely fallen apart in my first bout. He walked toward me with heavy steps and then sat down next to me on the floor. He didn't speak a word. I knew that he was upset that I had resorted to the type of behavior I used to exhibit on a regular basis before joining the gym. I knew that he had worked hard training me for that fight. I wanted to apologize to him, but I was unable to speak or even look him in the eyes.

As we sat there, side-by-side, slouched in the corner of the empty locker room, El Buho put his arm on my shoulder and sighed. "What are we gonna do with you, chico?" I was surprised at how calm he was, although when I looked up at him I could see the disappointment in his eyes. "We've got a lot more work to do."

At this comment, I forced a smile. "Si," I whispered. "I'm really sorr—"

Before I could even finish my sentence, El Buho cut me off. "I know, Paco. I know you are." And with that comment still hanging in the air, Coach Castillo stood up and left the room. I sat there in silence for the next hour or so.

On the car ride home, my dad was not as nice as my coach. He told me that the fire inside me was burning me to the ground. He said that I was blowing an opportunity—maybe my last one. Of course, he mentioned military school again, and as a result of what happened, he had me endure an exploratory interview with the provost at Hill Valley Military School the following week. A half hour with that guy grilling me about duty and honor, and I was looking to get back into the gym. I was ready to accept whatever work El Buho had in store for me.

Even a few weeks after the fight, I felt awful. Not only did I regret losing my cool and hitting the ref, but I didn't enjoy being written about unfavorably in the local newspaper. Plus, it seemed like I had just poured an entire year of training, not to mention psychology, down the drain. I was completely depressed. I was starting all over again.

Of course, I began to question whether the progress I had made in the past twelve months was just an illusion. I wondered if there was truly any hope for me. Having knocked out the ref and having begun to serve a ninety-day suspension, Coach Castillo suggested—no, demanded—that I make an unscheduled appointment with Dr. Colòn.

Dr. Colòn gave it to me straight. "Paco," she said, her voice not as syrupy as it was the last time we spoke, "you need to force yourself past your doubts and insecurities, especially those that threaten to make you lose control."

Once again, I fidgeted uncomfortably on her office couch.

"If you want to become the best person you can be, not to mention the best boxer you can be, then you need to need to learn to tame the beast. We need to kick things up a notch," she added. "That's what we'll be working on today."

We talked about the need to control not just my anger but, more importantly, my reaction to whatever it was that made me angry in the first place. This is the same thing we had been discussing since the first time I met her. Only this time, Dr. Colòn asked me to try a more simple technique. This one was designed to give me time to control my rage before I ended up acting on it.

Now, when I began to get a sense that I would lose control, when my blood started boiling and I saw only red, I was to close my eyes and count to ten. The only problem with this plan of action was that if I closed my eyes in the ring for ten seconds, I would get flattened. I told Dr. Colòn that, and she said she was going to speak to El Buho about it, and see if there were any boxing techniques that I could use in the ring to regain my composure. I rolled my eyes at the thought of this.

It was the following Friday night when El Buho told me his story.

He was closing up the gym, turning off the lights, ushering all the boxers out. Before I left, he asked me to stick around and help him with something. I think he just wanted to talk to me. "Paco," Coach Castillo began. "I spoke to Dr. Colòn today. We've come up with some ideas to help you stay cool in the ring."

"Great," I said, taking a long drink of water from the fountain near El Buho's office.

"But first, there's something I want to tell you."

"Okay," I said, noticing the seriousness in his voice.

He walked out of his office and stood next to the ring in the center of the room. I followed close behind him. He ran his hands up and down the ropes that surrounded the ring. "Did you know that I wasn't a gifted athlete growing up?" he said. I shook my head. The truth was that I had never even imagined Coach Castillo as a kid. He continued, "I didn't love boxing either. I found my way into the ring pretty much the same way you did."

"Through a psychologist's office?" I asked.

"No," Coach Castillo said. "But I had a father who thought that learning to use my fists in the ring would be better than using them on the playground or in the classroom."

"You got into a lot of fights at school?"

"Si. All the time," said Coach Castillo. "At school, after school, on the weekends. I was constantly getting in trouble. I was headed for bad things, Paco, and a life behind bars," he continued. "I got mixed up with a bad crowd, not unlike your brother. Luckily, my dad had a friend who was a guard up at Graterford. He took me on a tour like the one I arranged for you, so I could see where I would end up if I didn't change my ways." He squeezed my shoulder roughly, "I was a lot like you, chico."

It was all making sense to me. That's why he was so intent on getting me into the gym in the first place. I reminded him of himself. And that's why he wasn't giving up on me, either. "How old were you when you started boxing?" I inquired.

"I was older than you, about fourteen, when I first walked through the doors of a gym," he said. "And I didn't know what to make of it. I certainly didn't know how to box. But I worked hard, like you, and I made it, all the way to the PAL finals and the Olympic trials," he continued. "Then, I decided to become a coach. I knew that I had gone as far as I could in the sport. Now I can honestly say that boxing has given me everything, especially my sense of values," El Buho added. "But, perhaps more than anything, it helped me to control my own version of el fuego."

I smiled. Never did I expect Coach Castillo to open up to me so much, to share such personal information. Nor did I think anyone had the same problem as me. To find out it was my trainer was both comforting and inspiring at the same time—especially because the man I was looking at had total control over his emotions. This gave me the hope that some day I would as well.

"When I would feel my rage start to take over, when I would begin to sense that I was starting to lose it during a fight," Coach Castillo said, "I focused all my energy on dancing. That's what I was talking to Dr. Colón about today. That's what made me realize that it was time to tell you about my past."

"Dancing?" I asked.

"Si, bailando," El Buho explained. "I focused on my footwork until I was able to get back to executing the game plan that my trainer had taught me to follow. I can't believe it's taken me this long to realize that this technique can work for you. Our goal, Paco," he added, "is to never have another incident like the Godwin fight. Never. And, to reach that goal, you need to become a dancer— just like me."

I nodded.

"Can I tell you something, chico, and can I have you promise not to get a big head about it?" El Buho asked.

"Absolutely," I replied, completely serious.

He leaned in close to me. "I think you can be a champion, Paco. You have so much natural talent. I've never seen anything like it. I really believe in you."

"A champion. Me?" I spoke these words aloud and nearly cried. I never thought much of myself, but just knowing that someone, anyone, thought that I could be a champion, made me feel great. "Thank you." I whispered.

El Buho laughed. "But before we make you the champ, we have to make you a dancer."

I wondered how I would become a dancer. After all, I could barely keep a beat. Then again, I didn't have much of a choice: One more disqualification in a sanctioned amateur bout and I would have to sit out a year, not just three months. I was beginning to like boxing too much to endure a twelve-month layoff. Besides, if I wanted to become a champion I needed to get back in the ring.

At home, after dinner, my little sister tried to grab the remote control out of my hands so she could watch cartoons. I figured it was as good a time as any to put Dr. Colòn's most recent plan for me into action. Standing in front of Marisol, I shut my eyes and started silently counting, "Uno, dos, tres. . . ."

By the time I got to ocho, she was sitting inches away from

the television screen, watching her show, remote firmly in hand. And I was relatively calm. I still wanted the clicker back, so I could finish watching a couple of contenders battle it out for a piece of the middleweight title. The rage that was building inside of me, though, had subsided.

I smiled. Okay, that kind of worked, I thought. I didn't know if it would be successful when I faced a more serious situation—more serious than my kid sister. I wondered if I could pull it off when someone infuriated me to the point that all I wanted to do was knock them senseless. I decided that it would certainly be worth a try.

The following night, back in the gym, forcing myself to dance when all I wanted to do was flail away, was a lot tougher. For one thing, I wasn't the most graceful guy in the gym. At thirteen years old, I was still learning how to box—from the bottom up. Footwork in the ring did not come as easily to me as punching did. And yet, as Coach Castillo reminded me constantly, it was a basic component of a boxer's potential for success.

According to El Buho, being light on my feet was key. It would allow me to not only attack, but also defend from a balanced position at any time. I was great at attacking. My natural instincts allowed me to throw quick and powerful combinations. But if I wasn't light on my feet, bigger opponents would trade punches with me until I hit the floor. That wouldn't get me where I wanted to be.

In addition to practicing moving my feet over and over again, I was learning how to avoid crossing them and tripping. Although advantageous in many other sports, crossing one's feet is dangerous in boxing. "You get hit while your feet are crossed," Coach

Castillo said, "and you're not going to get up."

I understood that, but I didn't much like the idea of backpedaling. I explained to my trainer that it wasn't in my makeup to retreat. "You've got tenacity and persistence. I haven't seen many boxers your age with your heart," Coach Castillo said. "You never back up, that's true. But while it's admirable, it's also dangerous," he added. "Unless you know exactly what you're doing, and what you intend to do, it will backfire on you—and you'll suffer because of it. How well you move on your feet, both from side to side and from front to back, will determine how well you can use that tenacity as a competitive advantage," he continued, "and how quickly you're able to control el fuego."

So I learned to dance. In three short months, which felt like five years, I learned how to keep my weight balanced and how to stay on the balls of my feet so I could quickly spin or retreat to safety whenever necessary. When I finally stepped into the ring with a sparring partner, it felt like he was moving in slow motion. I confessed this to El Buho, who simply smiled. "Imagine what you look like to him, chico. You're gonna be a ghost out there. They won't be able to touch you."

From that day forward, Coach Castillo had me practice my movements as he took on the role of my opponent. We did this for hours every day before we started working on my punching and weight training. He had me shift and shuffle my feet quickly, always remembering to keep them close to the ground. His explanation was that by establishing a solid base under me, I would be less vulnerable to being caught flat-footed on counterpunches.

We tweaked everything about my movements during those three months. He had me switch stances, changing which foot I put in front. And he had me working my calf muscles by jumping rope, riding the gym's stationary bike and doing numerous bag drills. All the while, I'd be moving constantly. "Your movement, your punches and your strategy all have to be in sync," El Buho said, "so you need to constantly be thinking about your footwork. Also, this will distract you from feeling angry or out of control."

From time to time he would lace up his gloves and get in the ring himself to spar with one of the other trainers. Man, was he smooth! He still had the goods. He'd have me watch from ringside, where I was instructed to observe only his feet. It was amazing to see El Buho in action. He was so quick.

After a few rounds of that, he'd invite me into the ring to learn from a much closer vantage point. As his sparring partner, I could no longer watch his feet. I had to watch his head, his shoulders, his torso, and his hands. And even though I thought I knew what his feet might do, I couldn't avoid the inevitable. I would end up chasing him around the ring, swinging where I thought he was. But I'd find out all too quickly that he had long since left that spot for somewhere else. He would emphasize his point with a flick of his jab, more often than not to my face. "Remember, a boxer with good footwork is exactly like a dancer," Coach Castillo would say with a wink. "Only difference is he wants to hit his partner." Then he would rear back and jab me in the head. Smiling, he would ask, "You like that, chico?"

CHAPTER TWELVE

TAMING THE BEAST

I dropped my next fight, but that was okay. At least I didn't let el fuego dictate the outcome. El Buho said I had improved, too. Still, I hated being zero and two. I wanted to win one so badly.

Next up for me was fellow Puerto Rican, Virgilio Ortiz, who hailed from Trenton, New Jersey. Although he had yet to lose, this was only Ortiz's second amateur match, so I came in as the more seasoned competitor—by one bout.

The word on Ortiz was that he liked to sit back and let the action come to him; that is, he relied on his counterpunching ability. So the odds seemed to be in my favor. Ortiz was one of those boxers who regularly took two punches to throw one. His nonchalance toward pressing the action was something I could not identify with, my nature being aggressive. I was happy to hear that my job was to take the fight to him.

According to El Buho, Ortiz was the perfect candidate to jump on in a hurry—as long as I didn't make any mental mistakes.

Coach Castillo's game plan was for me to come out jabbing, setting up Ortiz for big hooks to the head, his reported weakness.

El Buho warned me, though, not to get lured into a false sense of security. Ortiz could be one of those boxers who liked to snare his opponent in a trap. His strategy could be to entice an overly confident challenger to come in nice and close. Once there, Ortiz would hit him with everything he had.

El Buho said he had seen it before, boxers who would let their opponents think they were winning by allowing them to dictate the action, then come back with a vengeance when the adversary least expected it. "I've seen boxers come out thinking the fight was theirs, only to have the other guy steal that particular round and then the bout," said Coach Castillo.

He said that the original boxer to perfect this technique was Muhammad Ali, with his famous rope-a-dope. Ali, "The Greatest," would lie on the ropes, letting his opponent flail away. While on the ropes, he would dodge or block most of the punches his opponent threw in the hope that, before long, his opponent would run out of gas. When that happened, which it did more often than not, Ali would easily knock out his exhausted foe.

Other boxers would try to copy what Sugar Ray Leonard did repeatedly in his classic twelve-round 1987 middleweight title win over Marvelous Marvin Hagler. Leonard won by tiring his opponent out throughout a round, and then throwing flurries during the last twenty seconds of each round, right in front of the scorers' table. "The last thing the judges saw was Leonard peppering Hagler with multiple punches," said Coach Castillo. "At that point, I bet they couldn't even remember what Hagler had done earlier in the round. The point is: be relentless in pouring on the pressure," he added. "But don't get cocky, and don't get caught. Move in and out without getting tagged." Now staring directly into my eyes as Henry Garcia put in my mouthpiece, Coach Castillo said, "It's time to punch your dance card, chico."

The fight was being held inside the local National Guard Armory. When the bell rang to start the bout, I did what I had been instructed. I moved in to establish my presence, and my left jab, from the get-go. I felt comfortable bouncing on the balls of my feet, sticking my jab in Ortiz's face and then dancing away before he got any ideas.

Occasionally, during the first round, I'd throw a hook in the vicinity of Oritz's head. I wanted to see if he was ready for it. In each instance, he was. My only recourse was to keep banging away, trying to score points. It was clear that at the end of the first round, I was in the lead. I had been on the offensive for the entire two minutes and, except for a few counterpunches thrown on Ortiz's behalf, I was the only one of us really doing anything.

That all changed in Round Two. As I picked up where I had left off, pressing the action, Ortiz seemed to come alive. When I backed him into the ropes, he shot back two picture-perfect punches: one, a straight right hand, the other, a straight left. They found my head and not only scored right in front of the judges, but stung a little, too.

He had gotten me before I could get away. And when I did put some distance between us, I staggered more so than danced. Now I was worried. El Buho told me to be aware of this and now it was actually happening. Ortiz was the spider and I was the un-suspecting moth about to be caught in his web. I was beginning to get frustrated. Every time I got in close to pop him, Ortiz would absorb the blow and send me on my way. The problem was, I wasn't leaving the scene because I had executed El Buho's plan. I was dancing away because I had stuck around too long and gotten popped. And the head shots he was nailing me with were starting to hurt.

It was a little more than midway through the second round, after I heard El Buho shout from my corner that I was getting hit too often, when el fuego first showed its colors. As a result, I started to lose all semblance of control—of my fight plan, of my body, and of my temper. I stopped dancing, which was the only thing keeping me from ending up on my back. Once more, I started to flail away, leaving myself wide open. It came as no surprise, then, as the second round came to a close, that Ortiz tagged me with a right uppercut that knocked me into the ropes.

Upon hearing the bell sound, I looked over my shoulder. I was leaning on the ropes exactly in front of the judges' table. Score another point for Virgilio.

In my corner, El Buho had to forcefully sit me down on the stool. My body was in the ring but my mind was not. For that reason, Coach Castillo put his hands on either side of my head to get me to focus. I was off in that place where I'd go when my killer instinct served as the fuel that kept el fuego raging. He had been talking, but I hadn't heard him up until that point. "Paco!" he shouted, slapping his hands on my headgear as he yelled. "Paco!"

I snapped out of it, at least somewhat. My eyes opened wider and my vision got a bit sharper. Staring into his eyes, I saw a look of desperation come over his face. "Last round, chico, and you're blowing it," he said. "You're getting suckered, just like I warned you about. You're losing your cool. Tell me if I'm wrong."

91

He wasn't wrong. I breathed deeply, trying to clear my head of the cobwebs. It wasn't working. "What do I do?" I asked my trainer.

"You move in for the kill," El Buho said, the look on his face turning to one of determination. "You feel that anger inside of you?"

"Yes," I answered, breathing heavily and staring across at my opponent.

"Okay. Now I want you to go into that ring and hide that anger in your feet. Don't let him see it—don't let him know it's there, or what's coming. Then I want you to dance around this guy until he is seeing two of you." Coach Castillo grabbed my head with both of his hands again, "Then I want you to take that anger from your feet, and I want you to explode on this guy!"

I must have had a strange expression on my face just then, because Coach Castillo nearly laughed. "That's right, Paco, you move in and you stay in," he explained. "You know now that he's going to fire back. Be ready for it, dance, and then explode. It's time. You're ready to use el fuego as your great strength. Just control it!"

Ding!

"Control, then explode!"

I went out for Round Three intent on beating Ortiz at his own game. I was more fired up and excited then I ever remembered being in the ring. It was like something had clicked—I finally understood that el fuego was both my greatest weakness and my greatest strength. Now I just had to control it, which was easier said than done. Bringing out el fuego too early, or worse, not being able to pull back once it appeared, would cost me the fight.

The final three minutes of the bout began as the first did, with Ortiz sitting back waiting for me to walk into a left-right combination. Control it, I thought to myself, as I danced in circles around my opponent. Control it.

I became aware that Ortiz was frustrated, as he threw one wild punch after another—none of which were landing. That's when I pushed forward. Only this time, I did so knowing that my opponent would throw a counterpunch which I was ready for.

After I let go with a jab-jab hook combination of my own, which Ortiz blocked, he snapped off a straight right. It was exactly what I thought he'd throw. I blocked it with my left hand, at the same time dancing to my left. This opened up a clear path for me to hit him on the chin, if I could uncork my right hand quickly enough.

I did. At that moment, I felt el fuego in my feet and was able to bring all of that stored strength and energy toward my right fist. Then I exploded, catching Ortiz with a hard right to his face directly in front of the judges. It was a clean and impressive punch, worth a solid point. And Ortiz grunted as my glove slammed into his forehead. He looked dazed.

I knew enough not to get caught admiring my own handiwork. I was careful not to stick around. Relying on my newfound footwork, I threw another two jabs before heading back into the center of the ring. I had the upper hand once again. I now had Virgilio Ortiz chasing after me. Time was running out for him, and he knew it, so he came in hard and fast. That was his big mistake. I was ready to do what I had wanted to do all night, which was tee off on him.

First, I backed him up with a jab to the head. Then, as he leaned slightly backward, I threw a sharp hook to the body. Although the judges may not have seen my second punch, Ortiz certainly felt it. It landed just under his heart, and I could tell it hurt. He turned his body, ever so slightly, and dropped his hands to cushion what he thought my next punch would be—a shot to his midsection. I didn't accommodate him.

By focusing all his attention on his stomach, he left his top half exposed. I capitalized, snapping his head back with a left hook, then a right hook. He covered up, then tried to tie me up. I would have none of it. I quickly went back to the body. I heard El Buho yelling at me to keep moving, just in case Ortiz was a better actor than he was a boxer. So I threw a few more shots at his face before dancing away to inspect the damage.

He wasn't out on his feet, but I could tell by looking into his eyes that he knew he didn't have a chance to win the fight. But he was a warrior, I'll give him that. He came in yet again. I figured his intent was to throw his arms around me to avoid getting tagged several more times before the bell rang. I didn't wait to see if I was right. I threw a crisp left hook that nailed him square on the temple. I knew it was going to be the last punch of the night when I saw it connect. So did the referee. As Ortiz hit the canvas, the third man in the ring signaled the end to the fight. I had won my first bout with a knockout!

I realized, as the ref held my hand up high that I never would have won had it not been for Coach Castillo. Without his instructions, and without my ability to dance, I would have lost that bout for sure. Ortiz was not a better boxer than I was. Had I been knocked out, which I very easily could have been, it would have been my fault. I would have beaten myself by losing control again.

As I walked back to the locker room with a record of one

and two, El Buho asked me how I felt now that I had that victory I so desperately wanted. "I was just thinking how much I like boxing," I said, "despite all the rules."

Coach Castillo laughed. "Yeah, winning helps you feel the love," he said, chuckling.

"No, it's more than that," I said. "I love the feeling I get in the ring when I know I'm doing everything right—when I'm in control of el fuego. I've never felt that before tonight. All the hard work and sacrifice is really paying off. I really controlled it, tonight."

"That's a special feeling," said El Buho, "and one that not too many people get to experience."

"I know," I said. "Once I did what I was supposed to do, my body and mind were like one. There was no way I was going to lose. I couldn't lose."

El Buho smiled.

"I've been watching Henry's tapes, the ones of the Olympic bouts that he lends to the boxers at the PAL," I continued.

"Yeah?" answered Coach Castillo.

"I think I want to win the Olympic gold some day."

El Buho put his hand on my shoulder. "And I want to help you do it," he said. "You know, Paco," he added, opening the door to the locker room, "in many ways, you're the boxer I was born to coach."

A few months after the fight, I sat across from JoJo at a picnic table in the prison courtyard, watching him finish reading an article about me in the paper. Since my fight with Ortiz, my record had gone from one and two to twelve and two as I won an additional eleven fights in a row! I was making a name for myself in the boxing community, and had appeared in the paper several times. When JoJo finished reading the latest article, he put the paper down and smiled. "Man, it sounds like you're on your way to the world championship, Paco." He punched me in the arm, jokingly. "You still gotta watch my left, though, little brother."

I smiled. It was the first time since I started going to Graterford that I didn't have to meet with my brother from behind glass. We were actually allowed to be in each other's company. We sat outside, enclosed in a small picnic area, where prisoners who had exhibited good behavior could meet with their visitors. It was early April, and the sun already gave off the warmth of spring.

Being that close to JoJo, even though we had been talking regularly for quite a while, was wonderful. "So, you're really sticking with boxing, huh?" he asked.

"Si," I responded. It was the same question he asked every time I came to see him. "It's one of the best things in my life right now."

JoJo nodded. "What's another?"

"Coming here to see you," I said.

I caught him grinning. "Well, I hope you won't have to do it much longer."

"What do you mean?" I asked.

"I just found out there's a chance I might get out of here soon," he said.

"Really? How soon?" I was starting to get excited.

"I'm eligible for parole in three years," he said.

"Three years? That's good, right?" Although I tried to sound excited, three years seemed like a long time.

"Well, that's a lot better than what my lawyer originally told me. My behavior has been perfect, too. That should score points with the parole board."

"That's great, JoJo," I said.

"Then I can come see you fight," he said, taking another playful swing at my arm

We sat quietly for the next few minutes, content to let the sun shine on our faces. Until JoJo's voice became more serious. "Paco, do you think there's any chance Dad will come visit me before I get out of here?"

"I don't know," I said. "You know how Dad can be. It might take some time," I added.

JoJo stared into the distance. "Well, that's exactly what I've got plenty of right now—time."

CHAPTER THIRTEEN

PUTTING OUT THE FIRE

Over the course of the next three years, I worked hard, both in the ring and out. When my killer instinct started to rear its head, I practiced dancing inside the squared circle and counted to ten at home and at school. The reward was that I just about wiped my bad record clean.

In the meantime, I was adding to my ring record. After that terrible start, I proceeded to rack up thirty-two straight wins. There were no disqualifications and no knockouts, my new-found footwork keeping me out of harm's way. Yet despite going to the Rock River PAL every night after school and on Saturdays, in addition to continuing my weekly appointments with Dr. Colòn, I knew the fire inside me still burned strong. Now, though, I was in control of it.

"Paco!" yelled Coach Castillo as I exited the bathroom, ready for my sparring session. "Weigh yourself first!"

Now a fifteen-year-old sophomore in high school, I had put on twenty pounds in the past three years, most of it muscle. It's not that I lifted weights or drank protein shakes, nothing like that. I was developing into a genuine athlete, thanks to the roadwork, bag work, and boxing I was doing. My body was sporting well-defined lines. No longer did it hide my strength; it actually highlighted it.

I had also become a gym rat. I was at my happiest when I was either training or fighting. I loved the gym. It was a magical place to me, one that captivated my imagination and made me feel special. Every chance I could get, I watched the other boxers go at it in sparring sessions. I would take mental notes on things that worked so that I could apply them the next time I climbed through the ropes.

No longer content to spend my time alone, I would also stick around after my workout to talk with the older boxers and trainers. I would often arrive early to do my homework at ringside, so that I could watch a sparring session between solving algebra problems and writing compositions.

My folks were happy, too. Not only did they know where I was every day and night, but I was keeping out of trouble and getting good grades. I even made the honor roll the second semester of my first year at Rock River High. For that, my dad told me that he had thrown out the brochure for Hill Valley Military School.

My changing physique meant I was moving up, yet again, in weight class. My next fight would have me in against a 135-pound eighteen-year-old Philadelphia slugger named Anthony Watts, who boasted an unblemished record.

"Just climbing into the ring shows courage and discipline, Paco," said Coach Castillo as he taped my hands before my bout with Watts. "But courage is fairly common among boxers. You want to be uncommon. In boxing, Paco, you have to train your body and your mind to accept pain. I think we've done that. Now we're ready to take your game to the next level. This will be your toughest fight." He glanced up to make sure I was paying attention. "Remember, boxing is one of the few sports where the stronger will consistently overcomes the better skill. What you don't have in skills, you make up for in heart. That's the mark of a champion. This guy may be bigger than you," Coach added, "but I'm guessing he doesn't have your smarts, your instincts, or your heart. Now, go out there and prove me right."

As Henry Garcia held up the middle rope for me to climb through, I scanned the crowd inside the legendary Blue Horizon in North Philadelphia. This was my first fight in a real boxing hall, voted by *Ring* magazine to be the top prizefighting venue in the country. Even more important, was the fact that this was my first bout in the prestigious Middle Atlantic Association PAL tournament. This was the tournament that El Buho had won a thousand years ago, on his way to pursuing an Olympic dream that wasn't fulfilled. Part of the reason I wanted to get to the Olympics so much was for my coach. Together, we had the chance to accomplish the goal he had set for himself when he was a young man.

It had to be close to 100 degrees inside the Blue Horizon that night in late March, but I didn't care. I was ready to show my dad, my coach and everyone else in the old auditorium that I had what it took to beat Anthony Watts. Granted, I was only sixteen and not as seasoned as Watts. But I had logged more time in the gym than anyone else at the Rock River PAL. I had paid my dues, and this was to be my coming out party.

Glancing toward ringside, I noticed the press. Never had I seen so many reporters and photographers. I knew they were here to see the up-and-coming Watts, whose name was already becoming a household one in fight-crazy Philly.

I danced a bit while waiting for Watts to join me in the ring. I knew he was making his way when the entire crowd turned to watch him swagger toward the ring. After ascending the steps, he jumped clear over the ropes, landed on his feet and basked in the thunderous ovation he received. "Don't let him psyche you out, Paco," said El Buho. "Fight your fight."

I nodded as Henry slipped my mouthpiece past my teeth and tightened my headgear. He held his hand on the back of my neck as he walked me to the center of the ring. Waiting there for Watts, I looked up into the balcony, which literally hung over the ring. It was as if you could reach up and touch the fans. I heard a couple of them giving it to me. They let me know in no uncertain terms that they were there to see Watts flatten me inside of one round.

I knew I had to block them out, not let them get into my head. I knew I couldn't let my killer instinct get the best of me and cause me to lose. Getting hit by a solid punch—that I could deal with—but succumbing to my demons was inexcusable, especially after all the work I had put into getting to this point. Still, listening to that crowd boo me, and watching Watts showboat around the ring was starting to make me angry.

Watts sauntered up to me and sneered. He kept that look on his face while the referee gave us our instructions, only he inched closer and closer, so that his face was nearly touching mine. His breath stunk, and he knew it. That's why he breathed heavily right into my nose. He was trying to intimidate me. I started dancing a bit more, turning my focus away from his bad breath and onto my footwork. I was looser than he thought I'd be, and it took him off guard.

After touching gloves and returning to our respective corners, we stared at each other one last time before the bell rang. He blew a sarcastic kiss to me. I ignored him.

It was time to get it on.

Ding!

We both came out somewhat cautiously, taking a few moments to circle each other in the center of the ring in an effort to feel each other out. The report on Watts was that he had a big left hook, but didn't use it as much as he should. He had a reputation as a headhunter when he should have gone to the body more. My plan was to stay agile and at least an arm's length away. Dart in, throw combinations and get out. Wear him down, then move in for the kill.

As we threw a couple punches in each other's direction, more for effect than for anything else, I thought about what Coach Castillo had told me back at the PAL. "Your hands must exploit the openings in the same split second that your eyes find them," he lectured. "But don't forget, while you're trying to do that, you cannot neglect your defense. Like a chess match, you let your guard down, and it could be over pretty quick."

So, just like in the Ortiz fight, I readied myself for a shot to the head as I looked for an opportunity to counter. I didn't have to wait long. Watts threw his trademark right, straight at my head. I sidestepped the punch, feeling the wind it generated as it grazed my ear. I shuffled my feet ever so slightly, planted them, and came back with a right of my own—a hook to the body. I caught Watts in the abdomen, a nice power punch that must have hurt. He looked surprised by my skilled maneuvering.

I didn't stop there. Although the game plan was to stick and move, having landed a power punch without much trouble so early in the fight led me to believe I could do some additional damage. So I moved closer to engage in a little inside fighting. After missing with a left uppercut to the chin, I swung and missed with a right cross. Although I kept my elbow bent, low and in tight, I neglected to snap my shoulder forward and up. This mistake guaranteed that my uppercut would land short of its target. As a result, I was off-balance, which is why the right hand I threw at Watts' head missed as well.

Watts was good on his feet, too, dodging my punches with skilled head movement. If his stomach was bothering him, he didn't show it. I thought he might try to tie me up, take a few seconds to get his wind back, but he apparently didn't need it.

In textbook fashion, after having missed twice, I was wide open, and Watts took advantage. He drilled me with a left-right combination to the nose that I had no hope of deflecting. The punches knocked me backward. At that moment, I felt like a cartoon character who just had his face flattened with a frying pan.

There was still time left in the first round and already I was in trouble. I began to lose control. The sight of my own blood, trickling down my chin onto my tank top, did it. Coach Castillo and Henry could sense it. Over the roar of the crowd, I could hear them yelling at me to keep my cool. But between the cobwebs I was feeling from the one-two by Watts, and the rage that was beginning to cloud my judgment, I dismissed their pleas. I thought I was better than Watts, and I knew I could inflict as much pain on him as he could on me. More even.

Such thoughts began to consume me, in effect trashing precisely what I had been fighting against for years. I wiped my nose with my glove, smearing blood across my cheek. Moving forward again, I threw about six or seven punches that weren't even close. I was punching as hard and as fast as I could, but to no avail. My game plan had gone out the window and I was getting beaten badly.

In throwing punches wildly, I neglected my defense, walking straight into a left jab, delivered perfectly in corkscrew fashion from Watts' shoulder. Rotating his fist upon reaching full extension, he snapped my neck back like a bobble head doll. Now I was truly hurt and unsure of what to do. I caught a glimpse of Dr. Colòn, sitting next to my father, at ringside, and it all came back to me. "Dance, Paco," I said to myself. "Start dancing."

I got on my bicycle, doing my version of the "Ali Shuffle," trying my best to move my feet in a dazzling blur. I had spent so much time practicing my footwork in the gym that I truly was lightning fast. This was the only reason that I survived the round. Watts simply couldn't catch me.

"Que haces, Paco? What's going on out there?" Coach Castillo asked me as I sat down on the stool between rounds. "You had me worried."

"Y yo tambien," said Henry, squeezing water from over my head and down my back before wiping my bloody nose with a towel. "Me too."

"I almost went to that place again," I said.

"But you didn't," El Buho answered.

"No, I didn't." I replied.

"Good. You're learning. And now you've got Watts thinking. He's in for a long night, wouldn't you say?"

"Si," I answered with a determined tone in my voice.

"And now you know that if he hits you again, which he will, he's not going to knock you down," said Coach Castillo. "Do the opposite of what your instinct might tell you. Don't stand there and trade punches with him. Keep making him come after you. Pick your shots. That's how you'll win. Comprende, chico?"

I nodded. I was ready. I stood up for the start of Round Two.

"Remember the good doctor's quote, Paco," El Buho said as he glanced behind him at Dr. Colòn, "most of the time it's not practical to be mad in the ring."

Ding!

The funny thing, heading out for the second round, was that I remember thinking how I wasn't mad. Not anymore. It didn't matter that Anthony Watts had bloodied my face. I was focused on my task at hand. It seems I had, at least for the time being, put out el fuego—tamed the beast.

Round Two did not begin like the first one had. Neither of us was content to circle around each other, daring the other to throw the first punch. Now, it was really "go time." After banging at each other for the first thirty seconds of the round, Watts figured he saw an opening, and he moved in quickly to exploit it. I was waiting for him. I blocked his left jab, only to respond with a left hook, right-cross combination of my own. I tagged him pretty good with the second shot, but not good enough to hurt him. So I quickly got back on my horse and made him come after me.

I did the same thing five more times during the round—although my punch combinations may have been slightly different.

Left jab, right cross to the head. Right cross, left cross to the head. Left jab, left jab, right uppercut to the midsection. At the end of four minutes, I had a commanding lead.

In my corner, Coach Castillo met me with the biggest smile I had ever seen, like a proud father who just found out that his son was going to college. "Muy bien, Paco. Muy bien," he said. "Great round! You did everything right, from start to finish. That was the best round you've ever fought."

I managed a smile, though it wasn't as big as the one Coach Castillo wore.

"Listen to them," Coach Castillo said, glancing up into the balcony. "You hear that?"

I turned my head slightly to listen to the crowd. I didn't hear anything, really, because I was in the zone. Even when sitting on my stool in my corner, I was totally focused on my task at hand.

But with a little concentration, I now heard what El Buho did: the crowd at the Blue Horizon had turned on local boy Anthony Watts. They were booing him with gusto. And a good number of them were cheering me on.

"That's because not only are you winning this fight, but you're also uncovering Watts' weaknesses and proving how good a boxer you are," Coach Castillo said. "If you really want to hear them shout your name, go out and do the same thing you did last round."

I don't know what inspired me, whether it was the rush I got from hearing so many people rooting for me, or maybe the good fortune of winning under the spotlight of the legendary Blue Horizon. I wasn't sure. But I did what my trainer asked. I went out and kicked butt. Bobbing, weaving, dodging, and dancing, throwing a number of combinations, and a few power punches to boot, I handed a frustrated and deflated Anthony Watts his first defeat. I proved to be faster, stronger, and more nimble. And, as a result, I eliminated Watts from the Middle Atlantic Association PAL tournament. This was big news because he was supposed to cruise all the way to the finals.

The standing ovation I received as the referee held my hand over my head indicated that the crowd thoroughly appreciated the fact that I wasn't even supposed to last a round with Watts. I had defied the odds and won some hearts in the process. Although that felt good, it felt even better to know that El Buho was proud. He told me so as we exited the ring.

So was my dad, who met me at the bottom of the steps. He told me just how pleased he was, too, though he didn't have to. The new boxing shoes he held up for me to see, which must have cost him plenty, were indication enough. Over the last two years, Dad and I had grown much closer. Through my commitment to boxing, I had earned his respect. It meant a lot to me. Right behind my father was Dr. Colòn, wearing a smile even bigger than El Buho's. She told me the exact same thing.

It was the reaction of these folks—not the ones who filled the Blue Horizon—that made me realize what I had accomplished. Yes, I had won a fight I wasn't even supposed to be in. But more importantly, I had tamed the beast. I kept my killer instinct in check and did what I needed to do, channeling el fuego into a useful tool. And, man, did it feel great.

CHAPTER FOURTEEN

EL MATADOR

Paco "El Matador" Diaz. That's what the newspaper reporter called me in his column. El Buho got his nickname much in the same way, courtesy of a reporter at ringside who thought Felix Castillo looked like an owl peeking out from behind his gloves.

So, from the Watts fight on, I was known as El Matador, which in English means "The Killer." It was a deceiving nickname. You would think that a guy they call The Killer would be a powerful puncher who knocks his opponents out. But that wasn't my style at all. According to the writer, he chose the name El Matador because I reminded him of a matador in a Spanish bullfight. Not because I moved in for the kill, but because I was light on my feet. A matador, when fighting a bull, lures the bull in as close to him as possible, only to move away at the last possible moment. His quickness, not his killer instinct, are what he is known for.

At first, I didn't like the name, because the reason for it wasn't tough enough. Eventually, though, I grew to like it, because it had a bit of truth to it. I *was* like a matador. Yes, I had a killer instinct inside of me, but like a matador, I was able to keep in check. My nickname fit me quite well, highlighting the difficult road I had traveled. I especially liked it when a kid I didn't know came up to me in the hallway at school and said, "Hey, it's El Matador." And I got a real kick out of it when an old man, seeing me jogging on the street, would call out "Buena suerte, El Matador! Good luck, Killer!"

And, because it meant I was doing what I was supposed to do, both Coach Castillo and Dr. Colòn loved it, too. But, to further live up to my name—and, in essence, the reason behind it—I had to become even better conditioned than I already was. Even though I now had one win under my belt in the Middle Atlantic Association PAL tournament, it was only going to get harder for me to advance. I needed to become an even better dancer.

That meant going back to work in the gym. For the next week, from five to eight o'clock every night, after I'd put in a full day of school and completed my homework, Coach Castillo had me working on every aspect of my game. Following my run to the gym and a brief stretching routine, I did a little shadowboxing in front of one of the gym's three full-length mirrors. After that, El Buho had me move over to do some heavy-bag drills, some speed and double-end bag drills, and then some focused glove work with Henry. I would follow him around the ring, trying to land punches on the soft catcher's mitts he wore on both hands. After a short break, it was some jump rope, and then sparring. By the end of the night, I was wiped.

Throughout I would work on my footwork. Each day I'd work on something slightly different, never doing the exact sequence twice. For instance, I practiced squaring off against a southpaw, a left-handed boxer, on Monday. That meant circling to my left and throwing lead right hands. On Tuesday I worked on fighting on the inside with short hooks and uppercuts. On each successive day of the week, it was something else entirely.

As the week wore on, Coach Castillo reminded me to use my common sense. If my body told me that my daily running routine was too much to accommodate the extra sparring, I should cut back on the road work. Just for now, though.

I tempered my enthusiasm for kicking it up a notch physically and kept an eye on avoiding any potential injury. Already I had training sessions where my hands would be so sore after sparring that I'd have to soak them in a bucket of ice-cold water, burying them under ice cubes. If I could tough it out for a while, I'd lose the feeling in my fists, but the pain would go away. If I could do it for about ten minutes, my hands would once again feel soft to the touch. I could then eat my dinner without needing someone to cut my meat for me. What was more, I'd be ready to go the following night. This was the life of a boxer.

That Saturday I slept late, even forgetting for a minute that I had a fight that evening. Just the night before, Coach Castillo learned that my opponent—from across the Delaware River in Camden, New Jersey—was only recently discharged from a juvenile detention center. He was sixteen, with a record that had already garnered him headlines. These headlines, however, were not concerning his record in the ring—they were all about his criminal record. He was looking to get his name in the paper again, this time for knocking me out.

I woke up around noon and lay around on the couch for an hour or so, then ate some cereal and did some math homework. At three o'clock I watched part of an old western on television, before helping my dad pack up some clothes to give to good will. It was around five o'clock now, and time for me to eat a plate of arroz con frijoles and get ready.

My fight was set to go off at the Blue Horizon at eight o'clock, the scheduled fourth bout of the evening. At exactly seven o'clock, Coach Castillo dropped me off in front of the old auditorium in North Philly. Neither my dad nor Dr. Colòn were going to be able to make the fight. My mom never watched me in the ring. She would go to church instead during my fights and pray that I didn't get hurt.

That was okay. I had made it to the place where I was truly fighting for me, not for others. Coach Castillo reminded me time and again that such a realization was necessary to be successful, and stay safe, in the ring.

I ran up the stairs and headed for the locker room while El Buho and Henry, sitting in the front passenger seat, looked for a parking spot. I was anxious to get in the ring. I remember thinking that I didn't feel nervous or intimidated about squaring off against a boxer who had spent some time in prison. After all, had it not been for Dr. Colòn and El Buho, I probably would have been in a similar situation.

I did think about JoJo for a moment, though. I thought about his life behind bars and, to be honest, it made me pretty sad. But as quickly as the thought entered my head, it exited. I had to shift my focus back to the ring. Any loss of focus during a fight could not only cost me the victory but lead to an injury as well.

Coach Castillo helped bring me back to earth as he taped my hands. He could sense things. His nickname said as much about

111

his wisdom as it did about the way he fought. And his intuition was usually right on. He noticed that I was acting a tad too spacey, even over-confident. "Paco," he said. "You better wake up, chico. I know you just put in a great week in the gym. But, you don't know anything about this guy—other than he's already done some time. For that reason, I wouldn't be too sure of myself if I were you," he added, tying up my gloves. "Who are you to take anyone lightly? This guy could knock you out with one punch."

I remember thinking to myself that this wasn't the most uplifting and motivational pre-fight pep talk. But The Owl was right. All I had was a good amateur record and one tournament win. I had no right to be cocky and no right to be spacing out just minutes before a fight.

It was Coach Castillo's keen observation that helped me keep my bearings as I climbed into the ring to stare down Antoine Lydell. Standing across from him, I noted that Lydell was much shorter than me. I also saw that, behind the multiple tattoos that adorned the black skin of his upper chest and arms, he was much more muscular as well. And I confirmed that he was much more mean-looking than I could ever pretend to be.

The corner of his mouth was turned up, and as he breathed during the referee's instructions, it sounded as though he was growling. Like a bear. I wasn't scared, mind you. I never really did get scared. But I would be lying if I didn't admit to worrying. It wasn't that I was concerned about this guy possibly hurting me. I was leery about him boxing me into a figurative corner that would force me to lose control. I didn't want to have another setback. I was making wonderful progress.

The fight started out like my last one, the second bout in a row that began unlike the majority of amateur boxing matches. In most amateur fights, the combatants are nervous and well aware of the small window of time available to make something happen. So they start swinging quickly. By contrast, in a professional fight there's no such sense of urgency. Boxers in the pros have time to conserve energy and modify a fight plan, if necessary, over several rounds. In the amateurs—where it's now, now, now—you pretty much have to get busy in a hurry.

So, when Lydell came out slowly, looking to bide his time in order to land one big shot, I realized that he had a pro style. It was the opposite of mine. I was an amateur boxer, in many ways a classic one, and the rules favored my approach. One such rule was unwritten: the boxer who could rush in, throw flurries, build up points, and spend the rest of the fight running, stood a better chance of winning than his opponent. I had done pretty much just that in my previous fight, and it had secured my victory. I won even though I didn't really hurt Watts.

You see, in amateur boxing, unlike in the pros, the force of a blow or its effect on an opponent doesn't count. The knockout is thus a by-product of the amateur version of the sport. A punch that knocks a boxer to the canvas receives no more credit than a regular shot. It is scored as a single blow and does not necessarily make the boxer a winner of that round.

Such a scenario was tailor made for me and my dancing feet. But not for the crowd at the Blue Horizon. Oh, sure, the boxing purists appreciated a well-executed fight plan with lots of bobbing, weaving, hand speed, and footwork. But the rest of the folks—the ones in the folding chairs alongside the ring and in the balcony above—wanted to see a knockout. For them, a knockout was even better than an upset.

That's why the same folks who loved me a week ago hated me tonight. I didn't bring a big punch to the table. Luckily for them, Antoine Lydell did. The audience held its collective breath, waiting for him to unload his huge right hand on me. As far as I could tell, the crowd thought it was a foregone conclusion that the little Latin boy would get knocked out by his bigger and stronger opponent. They were clearly in Lydell's corner.

They ended up disappointed. Shortly after the fight began, I stuck my left jab in Lydell's face. I kept it there all night, setting him up time and again for a quick right hand to the head or right hook to the midsection. Then I would boogie away.

At the end of the first round, I had Lydell backed into the corner. I let loose with a barrage of accurate jabs and hooks, thinking that my opponent would have been better off had he stayed at juvi hall. But as I connected, I thought ahead: I don't want to overstay my welcome. Noting that Lydell wasn't anywhere near ready to fall, I hurried back out onto the dance floor.

Even the chorus of boos—which reached a crescendo after my latest retreat to the center of the ring—didn't bother me. I was in control, in more ways than one, and it was beautiful. I knew I couldn't knock out Lydell. I was boxing him, not fighting him—and I was winning.

By the middle of the second round, Lydell had stopped growling, but he was still breathing, though much more heavily now. The cell block grimace was gone from his face, replaced by a furrowed brow of frustration.

When the final bell sounded and the ref lifted my hand to the ceiling, I felt vindicated, as the crowd stopped booing to applaud. I was El Matador, a boxer, and a pretty good one at that.

"So, you're gonna win the championship of the Police Athletic League," repeated a proud JoJo Diaz on the other side of the picnic table. "Ain't that something."

"I have to win a bunch more times to get to the title fight. I've got a long way yet. Besides, it's just a local tournament," I said, trying to downplay the significance of it all, especially the fact that I had won my first two fights.

"Still, you're doing awesome," said JoJo. "All my boys here are rooting for you, bro."

"Thanks," I said. "Too bad you all can't be at ringside. I could use the fan support."

JoJo laughed. "I don't think the warden will let us take a field trip to go to the fights." I started laughing as well. "But I'm getting closer to that parole hearing."

"How close?" I asked.

He smiled, "Close enough, Paco, close enough." JoJo refused to tell me when his parole hearing was. He was trying to protect me from getting my hopes up, in case he didn't get let out. "Anyway," he continued, "when I do get out of here, maybe you could teach me how to box."

"I would love to teach you. But it's not all about your big muscles, JoJo." I smiled, "I mean, if you were to land a punch against a guy like me, you might knock me out. But, to be honest, I don't think you'd be able to touch me."

JoJo laughed, "I like that, tough guy. I like that attitude a lot. You bring that into the ring and you will win that championship."

"It's not going to be easy, JoJo," I said. "I'm still learning how to box, you know?"

"Why are you talking like that?" he asked. I could sense he was a bit irritated by my comment.

"I just don't want to set myself up for a fall," I said. "Everything's been going so well lately."

"Listen to me, little brother," JoJo said. "This is coming from someone who knows. Never doubt what you can do, even if, at the moment, it looks like you're not able to do it. I doubted myself, my strength and my faith, and let others tell me what they thought I should do. I forgot everything I knew, everything I had been taught. And I believed them. Look where it got me."

I didn't know how to respond, so I didn't say anything.

"You know, what?" said JoJo. "You're my brother, and I'm biased, but I'm proud of you, Paco. From what you've told me, someone with a killer instinct—a true killer—would never have the discipline to become a boxer. You've got heart, little brother."

"You've got heart, too," I said in return.

CHAPTER FIFTEEN

WHO'S NEXT?

Standing in the ring at the Blue Horizon, I blocked out the noise, which was coming mainly from the balcony above me. I focused solely on my opponent as the referee went over his instructions. It was the championship match in the lightweight division of the Middle Atlantic Association PAL tournament, and I had my game face on.

Across from me stood Sergio Campos, a tough Mexican-American from Atlantic City with a chiseled body and only one loss to his name. He was a hard puncher with fast hands and an even faster mind—a ring technician with all the tools to make his opponent look foolish. I did not intend for that to happen. I had come too far and gotten too good for that. I could handle defeat, but if I was going to lose, I would do so admirably. My goal, however, was to win.

I had compiled three more victories in a row to get to this point. I even won another bout, uncharacteristically, by knockout. I was getting better each time I stepped in the ring. My record, at 37-2, wasn't all that far behind Campos's of 42-1. This was the match all the experts were saying would be the best of the tournament, even better than the heavyweight bout scheduled for later that night.

My entourage at ringside—not counting Coach Castillo and Henry Garcia, who were in the ring with me—was at full strength for this fight. In addition to Dr. Colòn and my dad, two of my buddies from school, Ramon and Juan, had come to see me claim the title. Even my mom and baby sister Marisol were in attendance, for the first time. Principal Grace had bought a ticket, too.

About a minute before the bell rang I looked back at them all one last time. That was when I saw him. Making his way down the aisle and toward my parents was JoJo. I watched him as he approached my mother, giving her a big hug. Then he lifted my sister high into the air and kissed her on the cheek. Finally, he made his way over to my father. They stared at each other for a moment, before Dad pulled JoJo toward him. I stood there watching them from the ring. To be honest, I was near tears.

Coach Castillo looked over at my family and smiled down at me. He then slapped my headgear. "Focus, chico. They'll be waiting for you after the fight." I took one final glance toward the stands. JoJo was cheering for me louder than anyone. Our eyes met and he smiled. I never felt so happy in my life as I stared at him, standing there next to my parents, with Marisol on his shoulders. He had kept his release date a secret, hoping to surprise me as well as the rest of the family. Boy, did he ever!

I felt a surge of strength coursing through my veins as I looked back up into the eyes of The Owl. He gave me a nod of assurance and one final piece of advice. "Remember, Paco," he said. "The boxer with the giant heart is the one who never looks for a way out." Our eyes met. "You've learned to live with your problem, which is always going to be there. You didn't look for an easy way out. You've fought hard to keep it in check," he added. "I respect you immensely for that, and a lot of us in this building tonight already know you're a winner." He looked into the stands, "I want you to show your brother what kind of a boxer you are tonight. I want your best tonight, chico."

Ding!

Approximately fifteen minutes later, I stood in the middle of the ring, the referee holding my left wrist with his right hand and Sergio Campos' right wrist with his other hand. The three of us waited for the ring announcer to reveal the verdict of the judges at ringside. "We have a unanimous decision," the announcer said slowly, exaggerating his delivery to increase the suspense.

I looked over at El Buho. He winked.

"The winner, and new Middle Atlantic Association Police Athletic League lightweight champion, is Paco El Matador Diaz!"

The crowd went crazy as the ref raised my hand in the air.

First I gave Campos a hug, telling him in his ear how he had fought a great match. Then I threw my arms around El Buho, who I happened to notice had tears running down his face. Over his shoulder, I saw my dad applauding, my mom crying, and Dr. Colón and Marisol jumping up and down. But I was looking for JoJo. I found him, in the aisle, trying to get through the crowd and over to me. With his right hand over his heart, he pointed to me with his left. "You're the champion, Paco. You're the best, little brother."

I gave him the same salute in return. I felt so happy knowing that he was a part of our family again. Just then the members of the media, who were at ringside, muscled their way through the ropes and into the center of the ring. As several flashbulbs went off, a barrage of questions came my way.

"Hey, Matador, will you be back next year to defend your title?"

"What about the national PAL Championships next month? Do you plan to participate?"

"Then there's the Pennsylvania Golden Gloves?"

"How about the U.S. Championships?"

"The Junior Olympics?"

"El Matador, do you have any ideas about representing your country in the ring?"

El Buho jumped in and responded on my behalf. "We're going enjoy this victory. El Matador is going to spend some time with his family. Then, knowing this kid, he'll be back in the gym. We'll take a long hard look at how we can continue to get better. That's our objective, to improve," he said. "Of course, our ultimate goal is to represent the United States in the Olympic Games."

Then, turning to me, he said. "Do you want to add anything, Paco?"

I smiled up at him. Then I looked at the sea of reporters in front of me and spoke from my heart. "This is only the beginning for me, because, as you may have noticed, I've got this fire inside."

TEST YOURSELF...ARE YOU A PROFESSIONAL READER?

Chapter 1: El Fuego

What is shadowboxing?

Why do boxers put Vaseline on their faces before and during a fight?

Does a boxer need to control his/her emotions during a fight? Explain.

ESSAY

Paco talks about a time when anger used to control his life. Write about a moment when your anger got the best of you. What did you learn from this experience?

Chapter 2: Recess and
Chapter 3: A Bad Seed

Paco is bilingual. What does bilingual mean? How did he become bilingual?

Who is Butchie LaManna?

Why did Paco's parents send him to St. Joe's?

ESSAY

In Chapter 3, Paco explains that he admires his brother, JoJo. Who is someone in your life that you admire? Explain why you look up to this person.

Chapter 4: Killer Instinct

Who is Dr. Adriana Colon?

What do the Spanish words "El Fuego" mean?

What does Dr. Colon think that Paco should purchase to calm his anger problem?

ESSAY

This chapter displays how much Paco has disappointed his parents with his actions. Describe a situation in your life when you disappointed someone that cared about you. How did this situation make you feel?

Chapter 5: El Buho

What was the deal Mr. Felix Castillo and Paco made when Paco came into the gym looking for a punching bag?

Why did Paco continue to pound the punching bag after he struck it the first time?

Why did Paco finally decide to take boxing lessons from El Buho?

ESSAY

As Paco unleashes his fury on the punching bag, his natural athletic talent is shown in his actions. Write about a time when you discovered a hidden talent of your own.

Chapter 6: Fire Down Below

What character traits did Paco's dad think his son would learn from boxing?

Why was Paco nervous about adjusting to the rules of boxing?

Where did El Buho tell Paco he'd eventually end up if he didn't find a way to control his rage?

ESSAY

In Chapter 6, Paco furthers his reputation as a quitter. Give an example of an activity that you quit. Why do you think it is so important to finish things you begin?

Chapter 7: Therapy

When El Buho took Paco away from the gym, where did they go?

What did the prisoners call the block of prison cells that lined the main hallway?

Who did Paco see as he was leaving prison? What difference did he notice in this person's appearance?

ESSAY

In this chapter, we are taken behind the scenes of a prison. What did you learn about prison in Chapter 7? What scared you the most about prison? Why is prison a place to stay far, far away from?

Chapter 8: The Visit

Why did JoJo rip up all of the letters that he wrote to Paco?

Why did JoJo encourage Paco to continue boxing?

What scene in this chapter shows that Paco has begun to tame "El Fuego?"

ESSAY

JoJo speaks to Paco in this chapter about the importance of playing sports and getting involved in activities. Why do you think that playing sports or finding other constructive hobbies is so important? What sports or hobbies do you enjoy?

Chapter 9: Ground Rules and
Chapter 10: Out of Control

What two rules did El Buho give Paco for his day off from boxing?

What did Paco learn in "Boxing 101?"

How did Paco react to adversity during his bout with David Godwin?

ESSAY

In Chapters 9 and 10, El Buho continues to show that he is interested in helping Paco become a better boxer, and a better person. Detail a time in your life when you assisted someone. How did this act of giving of yourself make you feel? Why is it important to help other people?

Chapter 11: Dancing and
Chapter 12: Taming the Beast

How did Paco feel about his actions as he reflected upon his fight with David Godwin?

Why did El Buho think that Paco needed to learn to dance in the ring?

Who did Paco defeat for his first victory?

ESSAY

In these chapters, we get to glance into El Buho's childhood. Like Paco, he learned to tame "El Fuego" with the help of his family. How does your family help you every day? What are a few things that are unique about your family?

Chapter 13: Putting Out the Fire

Why is this chapter entitled "Putting Out the Fire?"

Why did Paco watch the other boxers train when he was in the gym?

Who is Anthony Watts? How many losses did he have before he fought Paco?

ESSAY

Earlier in the book, Paco disappoints his parents. By Chapter 13, Paco's actions have begun to impress his mom and dad. Write about a time in your life when you made your parents, or another family member, proud of you.

Chapter 14: El Matador and
Chapter 15: Who's Next?

How did El Buho get his nickname?

Why was the crowd cheering for Antoine Lydell during his bout with Paco?

Why didn't JoJo tell Paco when he was scheduled to be released from prison?

ESSAY

Congratulations! You have completed another Scobre Press book! After joining Paco on his journey, detail what you learned from his life and experiences. How are you going to use Paco's story to help you achieve your dreams? What did Paco teach you about the importance of controlling your anger?